Also by S. Kay Weber

Double Truffle
Spaghetti With Murder

Over-Easy

A Terri Springe Culinary Mystery (with recipes)

S. Kay Weber

authorHOUSE®

AuthorHouse™
1663 Liberty Drive
Bloomington, IN 47403
www.authorhouse.com
Phone: 1-800-839-8640

© 2009 S. Kay Weber. All rights reserved.

No part of this book may be reproduced, stored in a retrieval system, or transmitted by any means without the written permission of the author.

First published by AuthorHouse 7/31/2009

ISBN: 978-1-4490-0653-2 (sc)
ISBN: 978-1-4490-0652-5 (hc)

Library of Congress Control Number: 2009907093

Printed in the United States of America
Bloomington, Indiana

This book is printed on acid-free paper.

Dedication

For my beautiful daughters and
our mutual love for Door County.

windows, putting away all of his summer gear, as well as the boat and the pier, would keep Harvey busy while he held down the home front.

Emily had already done her part, stocking the place with provisions and supplies before the cold and snow was upon them. She had preserved or frozen anything they could get from their large garden. Many quarts of tomatoes had been canned, of course. Pears and apples, raspberries, and strawberries, bought at local produce stands, had been made into jams and jellies, with still others stored in the freezers for desserts. Emily also made sure she had plenty of staples on hand to prepare meals for visitors. Her freezers were full containing several good cuts of pork, including roasts, chops, and hams. There was also an ample supply of ground beef for burgers, soups, and casseroles, at least a half-dozen roasting chickens and cut-up fryers, three or four turkey breasts and two whole turkeys. Added to this, were packages of lamb chops and two large roasts. Different cuts of beef, including roasts, fillets and Porterhouse steaks (for special company), two large prime rib roasts, as well as less tender cuts, to be used for stir-fries and stews, were also on hand.

And of course fish. *Lots of fish,* in every conceivable form available in the area had also been stored in various ways. Harvey fished and clammed with his buddies and prepared all they could to store in the freezers as they got ready to 'hunker down,' as Terri's father liked to put it. To go along with main course foods, squashes, pumpkins, potatoes, yams, carrots, and onions, were all stored in an old-fashioned root cellar. There were also frozen green beans, peas, and corn, stuffed green peppers, and red, green, and yellow peppers diced or sliced, ready to quickly grab for recipes as needed. Emily also kept an ample supply of breakfast items on hand such as several packages of smoky bacon, sausages, sliced and diced ham for frittatas and casseroles, and plenty of fresh eggs. No one was more prepared for the winter months, than the hospitable Emily Springe for company and overnight guests, especially her children.

Terri often told her parents they reminded her of 'Ma and Pa Ingalls' of the Little House on the Prairie fame. Of course, Ma Ingalls had not had the luxury of a fantastic kitchen with all the latest appliances to prepare everything and two huge freezers and a beautiful pantry to store it all in. Emily loved her kitchen and loved to have visitors. She and Harvey entertained often. But feeding her children and whoever they brought with them when they came home, made her the happiest of all. Of course, she had passed these strong maternal instincts down to her eldest child.

Terri and her business partner, Brianna, had their own store back in Boston. Terri's Table (& Specialty Foods Shop) was also outfitted with all the latest appliances and conveniences. It had been difficult to leave but they had hired five new employees to keep up the regular meal deliveries and take care of customers who came into the store. It being just before the holiday rush, the party tray preparation was down to a minimum, for now. Thus, Terri and Brianna were able to get away without too many complications and their employees were more than capable of handling things until they returned.

The girls were also, at this time, deep in the remodeling process of the rooms above their shop. Terri, Brianna, and Angie, along with their two *poofy* Rag Doll kitties, Louie and Maria, hoped to be settled into their new digs before the snows and cold came, along with the busy holiday season. Louie and Maria had been left in the capable hands of Amber and Kelli, cousins and trusted friends who owned the health food store next to their shop. Leaving *them* for two weeks had also not been easy and the cats were extremely 'put out,' to say the least. But the girls would be back soon enough. In the meantime, Amber and Kelli would give the demanding felines the attention they needed.

This long anticipated vacation would include many activities besides the wedding. There would be shopping, of course, along with boating, swimming, fishing, and any number of other touristy things to do. Terri was especially happy to have the chance to get to know her cousins again. But the *one thing*, she really wanted to do, was go to Cana Island. The last time they had visited Door County, the Springe family had gone to visit the historic lighthouse. Terri couldn't wait to get back there. She had especially enjoyed the pretty spot.

At the moment though, it was a beautiful morning. Terri went to the window facing the water and looked out at Green Bay. She her face and tried hard to recall what had happened. Angie waited patiently. Finally, Terri started to tell her the sad tale.

She and Rico had returned from a wonderful date they had planned for before she left on her trip. He had taken her to a fabulous French restaurant, and everything had been perfect. The food had been fantastic, the service top notch. The wine and dessert couldn't have been better. It had been a lovely fall evening, which would have made the date perfect. *For anyone else.* But that was the problem and it had been bugging Terri for a long time. Everything was just so…. *nice,* it was starting to make her gag.

Terri enjoyed being with Rico. She loved his kisses and felt safe in his strong arms. She enjoyed his company wherever they went and whatever they did. They had almost everything in common. But their relationship continued to stay the same and it was getting stale. At least he could have asked her back to his place so she could have told him *No!* But Rico had never even tried to, as they say, 'get to first base' so Terri could put on the brakes, tell him how she felt about her future and maybe even, *their future.* There had been no breakthrough, however, so that they could talk about it. As a matter of plain fact, Terri had finally come to the conclusion, that Rico had been doing everything possible to *avoid* any serious discussion in any way, shape, or form.

Terri's father had driven Emily, along with her huge pile of luggage, down to Boston the night before and she was staying with Brianna and Terri. So she and Rico decided to sit and talk in the car for a few minutes, before saying good-bye. Rico reached out and pulled Terri into a tight embrace.

"Mmm…..I am really going to miss you," he whispered in her ear.

"Are you?" Terri suddenly asked peevishly.

Rico pulled back from her and looked at Terri as if she had just slapped him! "What kind of a thing is that to ask?" She *definitely* had gotten his attention. "Of course I'll miss you! You're going to be gone for two whole weeks. We always have a great time together. Why would you wonder if I would miss you?"

"You know, Rico," Terri tried to carefully explain but she really needed to cut to the chase. She backed away from him and crossed her arms. "We have been dating for over a year now. We go out, we go to the movies, out to dinner, to baseball games. Everything just stays the same. We have a great time. But aren't we getting a little *old* to date like a couple of high school kids? Hell, high school kids have more of a commitment these days than we do, which may not always be a good idea but……."

"Oh, great," Rico jumped in and, of course, said the *completely wrong* thing! "Now it's all about commitment. What is it with women, anyway?"

"What is it with you, Rico?" Terri needed to finally ask all the questions that had been on the tip of her tongue for way too long. "Didn't you say a few months ago that it was time to move on? What happened to that? Or am I *just not good enough* to replace your *precious* Sandra?" Here, Angie jumped in, bringing Terri back to the present.

"Oh, my God, you didn't say that?" Angie was appalled at her friend's lack of tact.

"I *did* say that. And unfortunately, there's more." Terri went on, going back to Saturday night.

"How do you know about that?" Rico asked, looking as if he had been betrayed. "Listen, Terri, my past has absolutely nothing to do with you and me. I don't know what you've heard but….."

"*I know* that you were working in New York City when the Twin Towers were attacked. *I know* that you were engaged and your fiancee and her sister died in a terrible car accident. *I know* you have suffered great trauma and I am very, very, sorry for everything you have been through. But it really is time to move on and make an honest effort to *get over it*. And why *can't* you talk to me about it? When two people care about one another, they trust each other and hold nothing back."

Rico did not respond to any of her questions. So Terri decided right then and there, that she might as well follow her own advice and lay all her cards on the table. After all, what did she have to lose at this point? "I'm in love with you, Rico," she said in all sincerity, table and opened it. Brianna put down the basket she was carrying and Angie brought up the rear with the third one.

"I want to go inside the lighthouse first," said Terri. "Can you guys unpack without me?"

"I'll go in with you," said Courtney. "This lighthouse is practically in our front yard but we hardly ever come here. I'm anxious to see what they've done with the place."

"You guys go ahead," said Angie. "I'm going to just sit here and rest for a minute." She pulled a bottle of cold water out of a small cooler she had been carrying over her shoulder and took a swig.

"You wimp!" Terri teased. "When was the last time you took a nice long hike? Being a cop isn't enough exercise for you?"

"O.K., so maybe I'm a little out of shape," Angie admitted. "Sitting at a desk or riding around in a car most of the day, doesn't account for a good workout. You just run along, Sweetie. The rest of us will do all the work and get the food ready."

"Fine by me!" Terri called over her shoulder as she and Courtney walked toward the lighthouse. "Yeah, it's not like I spend enough time getting food ready, huh?"

"You love it and you know it," shot back Angie as she opened the basket she had been carrying, and started setting out its contents.

"That's quite a relationship you two have," commented her cousin as they reached the door. "I'm glad Angie and Brianna were both able to come, by the way." Courtney linked her arm through Terri's and pulled her close. "I've missed you so much, Cousin. I can't believe you're finally here."

"I can't believe it either. Oh and thanks again for having my friends join us for this vacation and your wedding, Court." Terri gave her cousin a squeeze. "I don't know what I would have done without Angie all these years, or she without me, for that matter. Oh, and Brianna has a story you wouldn't believe. I'll leave it up to her to talk about it though, if she wants to. Oh cool, souvenirs," Terri said excitedly as they walked into the bottom of the house.

"Natch," said Courtney. "It's all about the tourists. But it's neat to have the lighthouse open now. See anything you like?"

Over-Easy

There were lots of pretty and fun things to look at. Shirts, calendars, books, postcards, pens, pencils, stuffed animals, all the usual goodies one finds at basic tourist attractions. Terri chose a clear coffee mug with the Cana Island lighthouse on one side and the Eagle Bluff lighthouse on the other. One could never have too many coffee mugs, and Terri normally bought one whenever she went somewhere new. Suffice it to say, it had been awhile since she had felt the need to buy souvenirs so she planned to stock up while she was here. She also bought a dozen pens and a calendar for the shop, pencils and shirts for Jenni and Benjamin, postcards which were basically pictures of (what else?), lighthouses, and a book she knew her father would enjoy.

"Are there any other lighthouses we can visit while we're here?" Terri asked Courtney, as the attendant bagged up her goodies.

"We can go to Peninsula State Park. That's where the Eagle Bluff Lighthouse is and they give tours. It's right on the edge of a cliff and a really gorgeous place to take pictures," Courtney informed Terri as she paid for her own purchases. She had grabbed some pens and pencils to use at the B&B and a coffee table-sized book Aunt Susie had asked her to pick up to put in the living room area.

Leaving their bags of treasures with the man at the cash register, they walked through the rooms and looked at the pieces of furniture that had been salvaged from the past. The kitchen and pantry area held old jars, tin containers, dishes, wooden boxes, and pots in old cupboards. One room boasted the old-fashioned telephone with a crank, another old cupboard, and a table, perhaps used as a desk, making up the simple communication room of a century ago. Another room held a very old sewing machine, with a chair, and a small table. The bedrooms were very simple, the beds small, with perhaps only a small table and chair, rounding out the Spartan life that lighthouse families chose to live. There were also little spots to stop and read about the history of the area. Terri looked out one of the windows shaped like a porthole, at the calm, clear waters of Lake Michigan, seeing many boats and sailboats of all shapes and sizes. There wasn't a lot to see but it was neat just to walk through the rooms. Terri was also impressed to find out that the Cana Island

Chapter 7

Courtney was chattering away about all the things that needed to be done before the wedding and Terri was desperately trying to pay attention. I should have grabbed my calendar to write down all of these appointments, she thought. Dress fittings in Sturgeon Bay. Hair and nails at Courtney's favorite salon in Fish Creek. Shoes and hand bags to pick up, to go with the dresses. So many things to think about and the wedding wasn't even that big. Terri obviously, would need to focus on the food. The menu for the wedding was pretty well set and would be served by a local caterer. The family wanted to enjoy the wedding, not work during it. Terri needed to organize a schedule for preparation for the rehearsal dinner Friday night. She had promised Courtney that it would be elaborate and elegant for the smaller group. So there was a lot of work to be done.

For this comfortable Monday evening, the first of their vacation, the girls were sitting in cushioned lawn chairs in the backyard as Uncle Bill and Zach did the grilling for their supper. Emily and Sue were in the gazebo drinking wine, talking, and laughing, probably over some childhood memory, of which there were many. Terri sipped a glass of delicious White Zinfandel and tried not to think about how much she missed Rico. It was such a beautiful evening and she wondered what he would think of this place. There were so many fabulous views, hiking trails, beaches, charming little shops, and restaurants. Obviously, there were few areas more gorgeous than New England in the fall. Door County came close, though, with it's own special charm and it was hard to resist. It was very peaceful here, making it difficult for Terri to deal with the sharp outburst she had heard on Cana Island earlier. Despite Angie's determination *not* to get involved, Terri was having a very difficult time putting it out of her mind. It had happened and she had been there. She couldn't just ignore that. But Courtney was going on with their plans and Terri needed to listen and keep up.

"We need to go down to Sturgeon Bay tomorrow morning, gals," Courtney was saying to Terri, Angelica, and Danielle. "You are going to absolutely *love* your dresses. Angie, want to come with us?" Terri's hospitable cousin didn't want to leave Terri's best friend out of anything or feeling lonely. Angie, however, was *not* the lonely type.

"God, no!" she stated firmly and comically, making everyone laugh, even Terri in her misery. "Please, go without me! I will sleep in, relax, and read over coffee and enjoy some more wonderful food. I am on vacation and dress fittings are not part of it for me. I'm wearing a simple skirt and silk blouse for your wedding, Courtney. If it hadn't been for my step-mother, I'd probably be coming in jeans and a t-shirt." Angie took a healthy swig of Miller Lite and sighed. "Now this is living. It's like a paradise and I intend to take full advantage of it!"

"O.K.," said Courtney in good humor, "I'll take that as a no." Everyone laughed again as Angie sighed with happiness.

"What about you, Bri?" Terri asked her young friend. "Wanna come along and see Sturgeon Bay or stay here and be a bum like Angie?" Angie did not debate this point, merely took another swig of beer.

"Oh, I'd love to go along, if it's O.K. with you guys. It's fun to be part of a big family involved in such an important occasion. And I can't wait to see the dresses." Brianna and Terri's younger cousins were drinking Cokes and waiting to help serve the food.

"Good," said Courtney, "we'll go out to lunch and have a wonderful time. And I want your complete unbiased opinion of the dresses, Brianna."

By the time they had all recovered from their picnic at Cana Island, gotten up from their naps and met back downstairs, Sue and Emily were in the kitchen getting things ready for supper. There hadn't been time for a tour of the rest of the B&B as of yet. That would be on the agenda for tomorrow, when they got back from the dress fitting appointment in Sturgeon Bay.

For tonight, supper was all about typical Wisconsin foods. Brats and hot dogs, hamburgers, barbecued ribs, and chicken breasts were sizzling on the grills. They were keeping it as simple as possible for the first night's supper in Door County. Angelica and Danielle had brought out sandwich and hot dog buns, mustard, ketchup, chopped onions, Aunt Susie's homemade relishes, pickles, and potato chips. There was extra barbecue sauce for the ribs and mayo or ranch dressing for the chicken breasts. There was also a beautiful platter of cheeses, pate, crackers, and fresh fruits that Terri herself had put together for all to enjoy with their drinks before dinner.

Terri felt like all she had done was eat since they had gotten there. "I am going to put on weight on this vacation," she complained as a platter piled with grilled meats was placed on the table.

"Oh, shush up and eat!" Angie said, grabbing a burger and a nearby ketchup bottle. "We'll hike and swim enough for you to keep your girlish figure. You know you have a high metabolism anyway. I'm the one who's gonna get fat." She bit into the burger and rolled her eyes. "Whoa, it will be worth it though, with all this yummy food. Mmmm…..I think I had better try one of these brats, too. I don't think I've ever had one. Definitely *not* your typical Boston fare. This might just be worth getting fat over!" She took a bite and rolled her eyes with pleasure.

"Oh, blah, blah, blah," Terri said, and everyone laughed again. She chose a grilled chicken breast off of the platter and placed it into a sandwich bun. Adding pickles and mayo to the juicy chicken, she too, took a generous bite and had to agree with Angie. Well, what was a vacation about anyway? It had been a long time since she had let people wait on her this much. It was nice. "O.K., I guess I had better try one of these brats too then." Terri took one off of the platter and reached for a bun and a bottle of honey mustard.

"We grill the brats and hot dogs and then soak them in beer and onions," Uncle Bill informed them. "I'm glad you girls are enjoying them. Wait until we take you for one of our famous fish boils!"

Terri was looking forward to trying everything and learning all about Midwest fare. She loved being involved in food service, making her customers lives easier by providing wholesome meals for their families. The business she and Brianna had established over a year ago, was growing by leaps and bounds.

She had started 'Terri's Table' on a pretty small scale by herself when she had first moved to Boston. She had prepared meals in a restaurant where she worked part time. She then delivered them to the homes of busy families four times a week. Meeting Brianna, even though the circumstances had been really horrible at the time, had been one of the best things that had ever happened to Terri. It had also been the best thing for Brianna. She had lost her dear grandfather and was now estranged from her mentally ill mother, as the horrific events had unfolded. Yet she and Terri had met as a result and formed a partnership, as well as a close friendship that had enriched both of their lives and then some.

Now, here they were, on vacation in Door County and it was a perfect evening. Zach and Uncle Bill were done grilling and had joined Emily and Sue in the gazebo with their plates. Courtney and Angie were involved in deep conversation about what it was like to be a police officer. Terri could see that Angie was in her element. Angie *was* a good police officer. She was not a bragger about her job, however. She took her position as a public servant very seriously and was answering Courtney's questions in a knowledgeable, yet interesting, way. Brianna, Danielle, and Angelica were talking and laughing like teenagers as they cleaned up the tables, making Terri relax and smile, happy that her young friend was enjoying herself.

"I'm going to walk out on the pier, guys," Terri made the decision and didn't even check to see if anyone was paying attention. The bottle of White Zinfandel was sitting on the bar, so she refilled her glass.

At another picnic table, several relatives, including Uncle Bill's brother and his wife, along with their son and daughter, were also enjoying their meal and drinks. They also had taken a two week vacation for the wedding but were staying in a condo in another part of Sister Bay. Courtney's fiance, Jared, would not be making an appearance until the weekend, as he worked down in Milwaukee for a law firm. A lawyer! Whoa! Now there was a coup, Terri had thought when Courtney had first told her about her future husband. Maybe I should hold out for a lawyer or a doctor, she thought.

Terri walked out onto the pier and sat on the same bench she and Angie had sat on that morning with their coffee. The moon was almost full and Terri was enjoying the peace. The background noises of people visiting and eating sounded like a low hum. The water washing up on the shore made a pleasant swishing sound. Terri could feel herself nodding off as she was being mesmerized by the quiet night sounds. She placed her empty wine glass on the nearby table, lest she drop it, and looked up at the moon again. It hardly seemed as if it could get any better than this to Terri, even though Rico was not here with her. She missed him so much already, the rat! He could have at least called her by now. Maybe he had and she should go check. Her cell phone was in her room. She had not felt the urgent need to carry it around with her constantly, like she normally did.

She sighed and stretched, figuring she might as well get ready for bed. If Angie and Brianna wanted to stay up and talk with her cousins, fine. Terri had taken about all she could for one day. Or so she thought. She was just getting up and walking back down the pier toward the house when a louder voice rose above the hum of conversation.

"Jonathan!" Sue said excitedly as Terri watched her aunt move down the steps of the gazebo to a figure who had come around the garage. "We weren't expecting you. Is everything O.K?" Aunt Susie moved to hug her son, and Terri felt confused as he gently, but pointedly, pushed her away. That was not the half of it, however.

As Jonathan spoke, Terri saw his face in the light from the pole overhead.

"Everything's fine, Mom!" He sounded defensive, yet guarded. Terri, on the other hand, was glad she was down on the pier away from the rest of the group. The first sound of Jonathan's voice had startled her so much, she nearly lost her footing and fell into the water!

"Geez, can't I come home a day or two early without you having a nervous breakdown? Zach, get me a beer, will ya?" His younger brother jumped up to wait on him. Jonathan twisted the cap off the bottle and took a long swallow of the ice cold brew.

Terri could feel herself losing control again and tried to search the darkness. She had to get back to the house before anyone saw her face or she would give away her shock. As others from the group gathered around Jonathan and started commenting or asking questions, she saw her chance. Moving quietly down the pier, she veered off to the right, around the sandbox, behind some bushes, over to the side of the house, and to the front door. Once she was safely inside, Terri ran up the stairs to her room and sat on the pink bed, trying to calm her breathing. Someone had seen her move away and run for the house, however, and Terri nearly screamed when the door of the bedroom opened.

"What the hell is wrong with you, Terri?" Angie asked, and then she saw her friend's face. "Oh, my God! Did Rico call or something? Why did you sneak back into the house?" She shook her friend's shoulder and Terri put up a restraining hand, trying to get her heart to stop beating so fast.

"Angie," Terri finally started talking but she whispered, like there was someone around the corner, listening. What was happening? She couldn't even go on vacation for crying out loud, without getting wrapped up in a ridiculous, complicated situation. "Angie," she started again, "that guy, Jonathan. *That* was the guy, at Cana Island. He was there, with that Ed Stone look-alike guy. He called him Johnny. That's him!"

"Your cousin, Jonathan? That's the guy, the young guy, that you saw on the beach at Cana Island, arguing with the older guy." Angie was making a statement now, repeating the words, to be totally sure she could completely understand what Terri was saying. "You are absolutely sure? No doubt in your mind?"

"Angie, for once, don't go all cop on me! *There is no doubt in my mind.* The voice, the face. *My cousin Jonathan*, is the guy, that I saw on the beach! *Now* what are we going to do? Still think we can't get involved?"

The look on Angie's face was one of surprise and then, frustration. Not get involved? Well, they definitely were left with no other choice now, were they?

Chapter 8

"Fine. We're involved, Nancy Drew." Angie plopped down onto her bed and gave in to the reality of the situation. "*But,*" she went on, "just exactly what do you think we can do here? We don't even know what in the hell is going on!"

"Well, we *do* know that Jonathan is up to something and it can't be good!" Terri paced the room and tried to think.

"Yeah, no shit Sherlock!" Angie wasn't helping. They *so* did not need this! These two weeks were supposed to be relaxing and stress-free. No complications, no investigations, and heaven forbid, *no body count!*

"Oh, so now I'm Sherlock Holmes, huh? What does that make you, Dr Watson?" Interestingly, Terri asked this without humor. Think, Terri, think. She tried to push herself to come up with something they could work with. What was Jonathan up to? It was obvious that it was something illegal. But was his *life* actually in danger? Did he need to be saved? Did he even *want* to be saved?

Terri suddenly realized, that she didn't even really *know* Jonathan. She hadn't seen him since they were kids. That was why she hadn't recognized him on Cana Island. She had never seen him as an adult. He was quite a bit older than the rest of them. The last time the Springe family had visited Door County, Jonathan hadn't even been around. From what she remembered, there really hadn't been an explanation as to where he had been. College? Working in Green Bay? Terri couldn't recall. She and Courtney had always been close but Jonathan had seemed like the 'black sheep' of the family. Now, she was more convinced than ever, that something was terribly wrong. And the little she could recall from when they were kids, was that Jonathan had always seemed to have an attitude, a constant chip on his shoulder, like he was pissed off at the whole world. Mmmmm..........

Ever since Terri had gone into Ed Stone's house after his murder, *without* permission to enter the crime scene, she had become somewhat of an amateur sleuth. That being the case, Angie could see her friend's adrenaline rush and the wheels turning in her mind as Terri walked back and forth in between the two pretty twin beds, and she *wasn't* happy about it.

"You know, Terri, when you first told me about what happened on Cana Island, you acted like you had seen a ghost. Ed Stone's ghost. Now, all of a sudden, you're as cool as a cucumber. Why the sudden change in attitude here, like you've got it all figured out or something?" Angie was confused, at least more than usual, when it came to Terri's famous 'instincts' that she and Brianna always teased her about.

"Angie, you know I *do not* believe in ghosts!" Terri finally stopped pacing, sat on her pink bed, and grabbed the fuzzy-soft matching pink teddy bear for security.

"Fine, then what do you believe in?" Angie asked absentmindedly, not really expecting an answer.

"Sense and reason, cause and consequences," Terri answered back. Huh?

"Okaaay....That sounds poetic," Angie said with a huge yawn. "What is that, anyway? Bill Shakespeare?"

"No," Terri came back with, "Johnny Depp!" She moved to the bathroom to wash her face and get ready for bed as she waited for Angie's reaction. It had been a very long, eventful day. But Terri had the feeling that, as troubled as she was, sleep would still come easily tonight. Angie was right. Suddenly, she did feel a lot calmer and cooler. Now at least she had something to go on.

"What? When?" Now Terri had her friend's attention again. Angie had seen *every* Johnny Depp movie that existed, even the really awful ones, and she couldn't recall *that* line!

"Johnny Depp as Ichabod Crane, in 'Sleepy Hollow.'" Terri grabbed a fluffy towel and patted her face dry. "Remember the basic plot of that version of the story? Tim Burton's version, of course. Johnny Depp played Ichabod Crane, who did not believe in any kind of nonsense, *or ghosts*, for that matter. He was no wimpy school teacher, however. He was a constable, an investigator, who felt it was important to *detect* what was happening. His character firmly believed in not just assuming someone was guilty, as the authorities were doing back then in the year 1799, without checking all the facts. So, the judge he challenged, played brilliantly by Christopher Lee, sent him to Sleepy Hollow to find out what was happening. You know, people's heads getting chopped off, that kind of thing." Terri took her p.j.s out of a dresser drawer and Angie moved to take her turn in the bathroom.

"Yeah, but as I recall, there was *not* a logical explanation," Angie continued the weird story. "The horseman was not only *real* but the story was creepy and kind of gross. Actually, Johnny Depp's take on Ichabod Crane was hilarious. He kept fainting." She laughed, recalling how freaked out they had been when they saw it in the movie theater. "Christopher Walken as the horseman was awesome though. All he had to do was growl and play his normally creepy self. That movie definitely gave new meaning to the old cliché 'heads will roll!'" She laughed again and then suddenly came back to reality. "So what in the world is your point, with all of this 'headless horseman' talk? And how do you remember weird lines from movies like that?"

"I'm not sure about that one. It just stuck in my head when I heard it. It really did make sense, though," Terri said off-handedly. "Anyway, my point is, now I know that what *I* saw was real. When Ichabod Crane saw the horseman, he had to accept it as the reality of what was going on and come up with a way to deal with it. That's the 'Legend of Sleepy Hollow.' That guy who threatened Jonathan was *very* real. He is *not* Ed Stone coming back as a ghost to haunt me. And you saw and heard the way Jonathan was acting when he crashed the party out there. I was hiding in the shadows, totally freaked out when I heard his voice and saw his face. But I did not miss his moody attitude. He even pushed Aunt Susie away when she tried to hug him. *And* he immediately acted defensive when she asked him why he was home." Angie nodded. She had also noticed the strange way Jonathan was acting.

"So, what do we do now, Terri?" Angie had changed into her jammies and crawled in between the covers of the comfy bed. "Or should I call you 'Constable Crane'?" She flopped down and plumped up the pillows before flipping off the light on her night stand. "If you're going to be a detective again, decide who you want to be. Sherlock Holmes, Nancy Drew, or Ichabod Crane, which one? Geez, I can't even believe I'm going along with this insanity again. Neither one of us should be investigating anything!"

Terri ignored Angie's sarcasm, not to mention her lack of support, as usual, and went on with her own thoughts on the matter.

"Well, one thing is for sure, we will need to stay very calm and not let Jonathan know, that there is something going on. Or rather, not let *him* know, that *we* know, there is something going on! We just bide our time, do what we came here to do, as in, vacation and the wedding, and eventually there will be a break in this case. From what I could tell, when I saw and heard the two men arguing on Cana Island, they've been at this for awhile. At least whatever *this* is, so something's gotta give, *and soon!*" Terri hugged the teddy bear, shut off the light on her night stand, and snuggled down under the covers. It was a nice, cool evening, perfect sleeping weather.

Angie sighed and made an effort to remain calm. "I'll tell you one thing. I absolutely *hate* your sense of timing. One week or so, one way or the other, and we wouldn't have had a clue that anything *was* up. We could just enjoy ourselves, no hassles. But nooooo! You had to end up, in the wrong place at the wrong time, as usual, and here we are, up to our necks in some complicated spy story, or whatever the hell it is."

Terri couldn't help but smile a little. She did rather enjoy the idea of an interesting but, hopefully, *not too* dangerous, modern day crime drama. No headless horsemen or creepy creatures. Just real people who sometimes, get caught up in really bad situations. There were a lot of weird things going on, in this day and age, *the 21st* century. Terri just happened to be around when some of it was unfolding, and right under her nose, too. Lucky her!

Chapter 9

The next morning, Terri got up early to help Aunt Susie and Emily prepare breakfast for the crowd staying at the B & B. She took a quick shower and tried not to disturb Angie. Angie, however, was not the least bit disturbed. She just opened her eyes for a second, waved her friend off, and rolled over to go back to sleep.

Their appointment for the fittings of the bridesmaids dresses was at 10:30. Terri had wanted to be up early anyway to get ready for whenever Courtney wanted to leave. She had no idea how long it would take to drive down to Sturgeon Bay. She had been much too tired to pay attention when they had driven through the city on Sunday night.

The beautiful kitchen was filled with wonderful aromas, the smell of fresh coffee, being the best of all. Sue was frying hickory smoked bacon strips, as well as preparing the Canadian variety. Emily was toasting English muffins and Danielle was preparing the juices.

"Hi, Sweetie," said Emily as Terri kissed her mother's cheek. "You're up early. And where did you disappear to last night? You missed a chance to meet Jonathan."

Terri chose a large coffee mug, this time, one covered with black and red squares and black and red checkers, simulating a game in progress. The words 'RELAX AND PLAY' ran along the bottom of the cup. One can only hope, Terri thought, as she filled the cup with the aromatic brew.

"How many different coffee mugs do you actually have, Aunt Susie?" Terri asked, putting off answering her mother's question about Jonathan, at least for the moment. She filled the cup, added her cream and bit of sugar, and sipped. "Mmmm….." she purred, rolling her eyes with pleasure. "What is it about that first sip in the morning?" She looked out the French doors, down at the pier and the sun shining on the waters of Green Bay. "Being here makes it taste even better," she added.

Sue looked at her sister and Emily shrugged. She knew enough not to push Terri, for now, not with a frustrating love life hanging over her head. Emily had said nothing to Sue about Terri and Rico. Her heart went out to her daughter but there was nothing she could do. It would work itself out, Emily was *so* hoping. She absolutely adored Rico and she knew Terri did too. But it was up to the two of them to figure it out. Or not. Interfering in her children's lives hadn't worked in the past. It wouldn't work this time either. Emily sighed and shook her head at her sister. Susie took the hint.

"Um, well," Susie said, confused but thinking about Terri's coffee mug query, "since you ask, I think I have anywhere from, 200 to 300 different coffee mugs. Obviously, every once in awhile, one gets dropped or cracked, so the turn-over can make the number variable. I think we stopped counting at 250."

At this, Danielle laughed. "That's one thing we are all trained to pick up, wherever we go. Anytime any of us sees a different or unusual mug, we just grab it to add to the collection. A lot of them are in the basement, Terri. We'll have to do the house tour later, among other things." She placed a pitcher of fresh orange juice in the cooler with the glass doors. She then grabbed chilled jars of homemade tomato juice out of the large fridge, to pour into more sparkling clean, clear pitchers.

"I can't wait to see the rest of the house," Terri replied enthusiastically. "Oh, and I wonder what our dresses look like. No puffy sleeves or huge bows on our butts, I hope!"

"Not hardly," Danielle giggled. "My sister has impeccable taste. I've seen the design. She was right when she said it last night. You will love them! And believe it or not, you *will* be able to wear the dress again. They are very chic and versatile. Courtney's dress is gorgeous too. We'll also go to lunch at one of our favorite restaurants in Sturgeon Bay. You and Brianna are in for a treat! I wish Angie would go with us, though. She's a hoot!"

"Well, for now, everyone's favorite 'hoot,' as you put it, is sound asleep!" Terri said with a little smile. She knew her friend and when Angie said she wanted to sleep, eat, and relax, she meant it! She had to crawl out of bed too many mornings before the sun came up, no matter what the weather or how she was feeling, to get to her *very* demanding job. Angie would take full advantage of this vacation just as she said she would and Terri didn't blame her one bit.

"Anyway, Aunt Susie," Terri gave her aunt a quick hug, "what can I do to help? I didn't come down here to just stand around gabbing. I need to cook something!"

Susie laughed and quickly gave her a job. "That sounds wonderful," she said. "How about you whip me up your version of a lovely Hollandaise sauce to go with our Eggs Benedict?" She handed her niece the perfect stainless steel sauce pan and Terri proceeded to her appointed task.

"Coming right up," she said, moving to the fridge for eggs and butter. It was nice being in a bright, clean, busy kitchen. Terri wanted to relax too. But that often meant being able to cook or bake and she was enjoying this.

Soon Courtney joined the ladies in the kitchen and also grabbed a coffee mug, filling the cup and gratefully sipping. Brianna and Angelica weren't far behind her and soon the large kitchen, was overflowing with busy, laughing women. Courtney put the two younger girls to work making muffins and mixing up pancake mix. She also informed the girls that she wanted to get going by 9:30. Obviously, it would be good to arrive early. The dress fitting would take at least

Over-Easy

a couple of hours. Then, after lunch, they would stop to check on the flowers and wedding favors for the tables.

"So, Cousin," Courtney addressed Terri who was carefully tasting her sauce, "what are your plans for the rehearsal dinner? You promised me a big surprise. Want to let me in on it, before I have some kind of a heart attack or something?"

"Now, now, my dear," said Terri soothingly, as she deemed her sauce perfect. She then placed it in the handy bain-marie, Aunt Susie had installed in the kitchen to keep sauces at the correct temperature. Terri used the one in her kitchen back in Boston often. "You must remain calm," she said, as she washed her hands. "All will be revealed in due course. Which reminds me, Aunt Susie," Terri went on cryptically, "I am expecting a very important, rather large package from Boston. It should be here sometime this morning. But before we leave, I will go on-line to track it. Will someone be around to accept it and put it in the cooler?"

"Oh, yes," Susie said. "Your mother and I will be here this morning. If you have an important package coming and it has anything to with this wedding, I'm not going anywhere until it arrives. I will even call you when it gets here. How does that sound?"

"Just perfect, like my sauce, as a matter of fact. Mmmm......" Terri knew that she was probably making her cousin a little nervous but it would be worth it in the long run. "Oh, and don't you two dare open it! Don't let Angie either. I shall inspect it myself, when we get back." Terri put on an air of nonchalance and refilled her coffee cup.

"You are driving me crazy. You know that?" Courtney confirmed what Terri already suspected.

"Oh, well, mission accomplished then," Terri said with a laugh, dodging a punch from the bride. "Hey, don't worry," Terri soothed her anxious cousin, "you will love it. Just like our dresses, right?"

"Fine, good comparison," Courtney relented. "O.K. ladies," she said then, "let's all grab a light bite. We don't want to spoil our lunch. Then we better get this bus moving to the big city!" At this, they all went for warm muffins or toast, with coffee and juice. Brianna slathered homemade strawberry jam on warm pieces of toast, with

Chapter 11

The tour of the Robertson B & B revealed more amazing delights and surprises. Angelica, leading the tour for Terri and Angie, started with the basement. The sleeping quarters consisted of three bedrooms, along with one full and one half-bathroom. All of the bedrooms were arranged for comfort. One room had two sets of bunk beds, fold-up cribs, play pens, and high chairs. These were put to good use by families with small or young children. One of the other bedrooms contained two full-sized beds. Emily and Brianna were currently residing there for the duration of their stay. The other contained a queen-sized bed and would be occupied by other relatives next weekend for the wedding. Each room had spacious closets, dressers, pretty lamps, and bedside tables. The closets were filled with comfy warm quilts, extra pillows, linens, towels, and toy boxes filled with colorful toys. There were bookcases and cupboards filled with books, puzzles, and games for every age, from baby to youth to adult. The basement rooms were decorated with a much lighter hand than the upstairs rooms which, of course, were filled with antiques and the more expensive pieces. All of the bedrooms contained T.V. sets with cable, DVD, and VCR combination players and stereos.

"This basement is huge!" Terri marveled as they went from room to room. "I don't see how anyone could possibly get bored here."

"Yes, we've tried to cover all the bases," said Angelica as they walked toward the back of the basement to the entertainment area. "As you can imagine, we have made use of Goodwill, as well as other re-sale shops. Mom and Dad have also found some wonderful pieces at our many antique malls here in Wisconsin. Moving, estate, and yard sales are good, too, but we always make sure that everything we pick up for the B & B is *very* clean and in good repair. Also, a lot of relatives and friends, have donated books, puzzles, and toys as the younger kids have outgrown them. We've built up quite a collection. I think we have every board game ever made! Not to mention video games for the Nintendo, Play Station, and X-Box game systems, which I don't even *try* to keep up with. They're *way* out of my league!" Angelica commented as they moved on with the tour. Terri agreed. She had watched Benjamin and Jenni play but had never quite gotten the hang of video games herself. Enjoying a favorite movie or reading a good book was much more her style.

Terri and Angie were awestruck as they came out of a short hallway and saw the wall facing the bay. It was completely made of windows and glass patio doors, providing a full view of the backyard, the pier, and the water. The house was built into a small hill that had been dug out to put in the beautiful wall of sparkling clear glass. There was a small patio, *not* visible from the back lawn where they had grilled out last night. Off to one side was a wall constructed of stone and a half-dozen steps that moved up onto the back lawn. The stone wall was topped off with planters and boxes holding more gorgeous flowers and foliage.

"Oh, Angelica, this is amazing!" Terri gushed. "Who designed all of this?"

"Mostly Mom and Dad. Uncle Donnie helped, too. My mother wanted all parts of the house to be accessible to the bay." Angelica made a sweeping motion with her arm. "With the porches and the basement, there are at least a dozen ways to get in and out of this house. One of Danielle's duties each night is to make sure that *every single* door and window is locked and the elaborate alarm system is in the afternoons. Sometimes Terri wondered when they slept. They seemed to have a never ending supply of energy and enthusiasm.

Of course, nutritious meals, beverages, and snacks were *never* a problem for Terri's crew. There was always plenty of food and drink for everyone and was one of the many perks of the job. All helped cook the meals and all ate. If they didn't get enough sustenance, it was their own fault. Naturally, Terri obsessed constantly about making sure everyone was fed, happy, and healthy.

Monica and Justine rounded out the 'Terri's Table' family and were currently working on a, make your own meals, project. While researching and trying out new and easy recipes, they were also checking into the purchasing of eco-friendly, yet useful, containers for the meals. The girls were also checking into marketing tools, as well as food suppliers. Kyle and Corey, of course, were always willing to try any of the foods the girls made and give honest and enthusiastic opinions. Corey and Kyle, had already accused Terri of trying to make them get fat. As fit and busy as they both were though, Terri saw no danger in that. They both burned up the calories as fast as they consumed them!

Terri was pleased with and very proud of her crew. Leaving for this vacation had not given her so much as a second thought of concern. As a matter of fact, she had been completely calm and thrilled as they had gotten ready to go. That was *until* that last night with Rico. Terri was trying to forget about him, she really was, but she just couldn't. She found herself thinking about what he would enjoy about Door County and there were so many things. *Too* many things. And if she didn't get her head out of the clouds soon, she would miss it all.

Mentally shaking herself once again and shivering, she forced her thoughts from Boston back to Wisconsin as Angie looked at her strangely. Or at least more strangely than usual. Terri gave her an 'I'm fine' look and walked out the glass doors onto the little sunken patio. They heard the phone ringing in the background and Angelica answering it in a business-like tone of voice.

"So," Angie was right behind Terri and *trying* not to pry into her friend's thoughts, "our second day is almost over. How about some sight-seeing tomorrow? And maybe a little shopping?"

Terri and Angie walked up the short flight of steps from the basement and were on the back lawn. "Yeah," said Terri, "if I'm going to send home souvenirs for everybody, we better get busy looking and buying, huh?" Walking over to the gazebo, she climbed the steps and sat down in a comfy lawn chair. "We haven't even seen the whole house yet."

Angie waited for Terri's next move and tried not to watch her friend too closely. They looked out at the bay and said nothing. It was very quiet at the moment. *Too quiet.*

So when an angry voice coming from the other side of the garage interrupted that quiet, it was surprising that they both instinctively remained still and listened.

"I can make threats too, old man," the voice said. "You're not the only one with a lot at stake here. And you are full of shit if you think I'm going to risk going to jail for you." Obviously, it was Jonathan talking on the phone to his old buddy Franklin. By the sounds of the conversation, things were *not* going well for their business relationship, whatever that might be.

Angie's eyes were huge as she looked at Terri who put her finger to her lips with a very soft, shhhh……. They both remained as silent and still as possible to follow the conversation. Jonathan continued to talk and move closer to where they were sitting in the gazebo.

"One more delivery and that's it! I say we tell these stupid jerks to go to hell. My sister is getting married next weekend and if anything happens to ruin her precious wedding, she'll kick my ass, or worse." There was a pause as Franklin commented on the other end of the phone. By this time he was yelling, making it almost possible for Terri and Angie to hear *his* reply, which was not favorable.

"Fine. I'll meet you on the island Friday night. You don't have to get so pissed off. You'll have a heart attack or something. Then what will I do with your dead old corpse? I got enough problems. My dad already suspects something is going on and will cut me off, *just like that!*" Jonathan snapped his fingers for emphasis and shut his phone, signally the conversation over before Franklin had another chance to reply.

Remaining as still as they could, Angie and Terri heard what sounded like a lighter and then smelled the distinctive smell of what could only be a marijuana cigarette. They could hear Jonathan as he took a couple of long drags, blew out the smoke, and sighed. "Shit!" Both Terri and Angie jumped as Jonathan swore and kicked a volley ball that must have been sitting next to the garage, off onto the lawn.

Finally they heard a car door open and slam, an engine start, and saw Jonathan backing an older Ford Taurus out of the garage. He got to the street and tore off down the road.

"Whew, someone just sparked up a doobie." Angie let out her breath as if she was near ready to explode.

"Yeah, too bad you can't arrest my dumb-ass cousin just for being stupid. Or better yet, maybe just to protect him from himself," Terri commented. "Well, this certainly clears up, uh, pretty much nothing, come to think of it." She scratched her head. "I can't even imagine what he would have done if he had known we heard *that* conversation."

"Hey, I thought you said you didn't think he was dangerous," Angie accused Terri.

"Well, now I'm not so sure. Did we, or did we not, just hear him threaten his old buddy Franklin?" Terri tried to analyze the little bit of information they had gotten from what Jonathan had said but Angie shook her head 'no way.'

"Hell, he was just blowing smoke, literally as it turned out," she said with a grin. "And in practically the same breath he seemed to be concerned that the old guy *didn't* drop over dead. I don't know your cousin Jonathan at all but I don't think he's a killer." Terri agreed with relief as Angie went on. "There is no doubt something illegal is going on here but I gotta tell ya' Terri, there's nothing *we* can do about it. *I'm not the law here.* Whatever trouble he's gotten himself into, it will come out and it sounds like *soon*. You heard him say your Uncle Bill is already suspicious. He's a pretty smart guy. Look what they've done with this place. It's amazing. Let him and the locals handle it."

"Yeah, I suppose you're right. But that stupid jerk better not ruin Courtney's wedding or there may be a murder after all." Terri laughed a little but she was only half-joking. Then she remembered what else Jonathan had said. "Uh, Angie," she started as a plan began forming in her mind, "Jonathan said they were going to meet on *the island* Friday night. Meet for what, I wonder. Mmmm…….and I think I know what island he was referring to." Finger again tapping on chin, she pondered the possibilities.

"Terri, don't you even *think* about it! No way am I going to let you go to Cana Island and get yourself…" But Angie was interrupted by a voice coming towards them. Thankfully, this time it was Courtney.

"There you guys are." Courtney walked up into the gazebo and grabbed Terri's hand. "C'mon Terri," she begged, "show me my surprise now. I can't stand it anymore."

Terri looked at Angie and got a warning sign from her friend. They would finish this discussion later! Angie was not happy. She knew Terri had her mind made up to jump into this investigation with both feet. But how was Angie going to stop her?

Chapter 12

Courtney was beside herself as she took items out of the box. "Oh, Terri, I can't believe this." She was *very* excited, to say the least. "Lobster tails, caviar, *truffles!* Oh my God! Where did you get truffles? And the most expensive kind, too. This is insane! Oh, and pate de foi gras. I don't care what anyone says about over-stuffed geese. I never liked geese anyway. They're noisy and mean. But I love the yummy pate! Where did you get all of this? *Why* did you get all of this?"

Terri just watched her cousin bubble over with enthusiasm. "You wouldn't believe me if I told you. But we have plenty of time in the next couple of days. Maybe we'll get to *that* long story later. So, what do you think of your rehearsal dinner being planned around all of these fabulous foods?"

Courtney grabbed Terri for a huge hug. "Oh, this will be amazing. Do you have all the recipes planned? How many lobster tails are there? What will you do with the truffles? This is Beluga caviar. I've never tasted Beluga caviar. This is unbelievable. When you said you would plan the rehearsal dinner, I never dreamed it would be like this!" Courtney was going on and on and Terri grinned like the

Cheshire cat as her cousin enjoyed herself. If only Jonathan would manage to behave for the next week and a half or so, this wedding might go off, 'without a hitch,' as they say.

At this point, Emily and Sue came into the kitchen to start supper for the whole crew and join in on the excitement. They helped Courtney look over the supplies Terri's employees had carefully packed, per their boss's instructions, and had sent from Boston, and were just as delighted and amazed as Courtney was.

"Well," said Emily, "it's about time I get a chance to get in on some of these wonderful goodies. Terri, you've got some planning to do," she said then, looking at her daughter with a raised eyebrow.

"Don't worry, Mom," Terri said reassuringly. "I've got all the recipes picked out and I think I know the best way to cook a lobster tail, not to mention the whole lobster itself. I better, considering they are practically in our backyard at home and I helped plate up like a zillion of them at Twin Pines. But yeah, the caviar, pate, and truffles are another matter. So what about supper tonight, Aunt Susie? What can we do to help? Oh, and has anyone seen my brilliant young assistant lately?"

"You talkin' 'bout me?" Brianna made her entrance into the kitchen just as Terri asked the question. "Oooo......finally opened the surprise package I see. So, you got a feast planned around all this stuff, Boss?" She addressed Terri and got an affirmative nod.

"But of course," she replied with an exaggerated, not to mention pretty silly, French accent. "One cannot be too careful, when one is working with *zee* truffles." Then she switched to a very serious tone. "So, gonna help me, kid?"

"I wouldn't miss it," Brianna agreed. "These truffles are fabulous, by the way, you guys. Like nothing you've ever tasted in your life. Just with scrambled eggs, they are amazing. You wouldn't believe the fabulous dinner Angie's step-mother, Judith, put together. And all I had were the leftovers. *Big, fat, yummy!*"

By this time everyone was laughing and talking and Terri was able to forget about Jonathan and Rico for awhile. They all began preparations for enough spaghetti sauce and pasta for a crowd. Emily and Sue browned several pounds of lean ground beef with chopped onions and slivers of fresh green pepper thrown in. Terri, happy to be cooking and working with virtually the same supplies she normally had on hand in her own kitchen, dumped several quarts of Aunt Susie's canned tomatoes into a huge pot, with tomato paste, tomato sauce, fresh mushrooms, spices, fresh garlic, and *freshly snipped* herbs. Brianna and Courtney prepared crisp salad greens, fresh cucumbers, green onions, and tomatoes. They mixed up savory cheese biscuits, baked homemade croutons, and pulled several loaves of garlic bread out of one of the handy freezers in the laundry room. There were plenty of pies, cakes, and cookies to suffice for dessert. Large pots to cook mounds of pasta were located and filled with water. Terri added a touch of olive oil to the water, added a bit of salt, and the pots were put on to boil.

Angelica and Danielle finally made an appearance in the kitchen, heading to the laundry room for fresh linens and towels to put in the bedrooms and bathrooms. They washed bath towels, sheets and colored clothes, while folding kitchen towels and sorting socks.

The smells of simmering spaghetti sauce, baking biscuits, and garlic bread, along with clean, fresh laundry, made for a pleasant atmosphere as the women worked, talked, and laughed. It doesn't get any better than this, Terri thought. She was especially enjoying seeing Emily and Sue together. They had always been close but yet so different. Thus their personalities balanced each other out perfectly, making them hilarious and enjoyable to be with. Terri couldn't remember the last time she had seen her mother so happy.

Finally, Brianna, Angelica, and Danielle moved to the dining room to set the massive table for dinner. It wasn't a 'get out the best china,' occasion but they would all need to sit at the large table to accommodate everyone. Durable, yet attractive, everyday dishes were set, as well as water and wine glasses. A plate of pasta, covered with tangy, meaty, spaghetti sauce, deserved a good glass of wine. Terri selected two complimentary reds, one Chardonnay and one Merlot, from Aunt Susie's stock of a variety of excellent wines in the basement. The small wine cellar behind the bar, which Angelica had forgotten to show them earlier, impressed Terri very much. It was kept at just exactly the correct temperature, of course, and was large enough to hold at least a couple hundred bottles.

Soon Zach and Uncle Bill made an appearance, ravenous and ready for a hearty supper. Terri was relieved that Jonathan was a no-show for dinner. She had no idea what to think of her 'black sheep' cousin and his bizarre actions thus far. She *did* know, however, that she couldn't just stand by and let him screw up his sister's wedding.

As they all enjoyed the delicious sauce with tender pasta, tasty breads and salads, Terri joined in with the interesting conversation and good natured teasing. All who drank were impressed with the wines she had chosen for the meal. Terri complimented both her aunt and uncle on their wine collection. They knew their wines and Terri was still in the learning process. Everyone enjoyed the dinner and the company very much.

But in the back of her mind, Terri was formulating an idea of how to question Jonathan without seeming like she was prying. An idea she had not mentioned to Angie after all. She just didn't know for sure how she would proceed or when she would see him again. He had acted very strangely when he had first seen Terri. Obviously there had been an attraction, albeit a weird one, on Jonathan's part. But Terri certainly didn't feel as if he was any danger to her or anyone else. But could she, maybe, somehow play on the attraction a bit and get him to talk? Ewwww.......would be Angie's opinion at this idea and with good reason. They were cousins, weren't they? Suddenly it occurred to Terri that there was something very strange going on that she just couldn't put her finger on. Why would her first cousin act the way he had? She had to find out and the sooner, the better.

Once dinner was over, Brianna, Danielle, and Angelica insisted that everyone else rest and relax as they would clean up the dishes and the kitchen. It was a cool enough evening for the gas fireplaces to be turned on. Terri settled into a comfy chair in the living room area with a Janet Evanovich paperback chosen from one of the many bookcases. Sensing that her friend needed to be alone for awhile, Angie joined the others down in the basement to watch movies and play pool. Terri couldn't concentrate on her book, however. She just had too many other things on her mind. So oddly enough, she *did not* jump out of her skin when Jonathan suddenly came in the door. On the contrary, she remained perfectly calm. *Well*, here was her chance after all, so she dove right in.

"*Cousin* Jonathan," Terri greeted him with a smile making her best effort to seem happy to see him. She was pleased, however, to see the startled look on *his* face, as he saw her sitting there by herself. "So, how are you doing this fine evening? Isn't it just a gorgeous night? I love this weather. Fall is my favorite time of the year." Terri knew she was rambling and didn't expect much of a response from Jonathan. So, she was surprised when he quickly recovered and sat in a chair across from her.

"Got the fireplace going I see. Yeah, it's nice out. Pretty typical fall weather here in Wisconsin." Jonathan tried to relax and Terri made the ultimate effort to control her amusement. If anyone ever looked guilty of something, *right here, right now,* it was her wayward cousin. She was also pretty sure he more than likely needed a buzz right now. Maybe he already had one? Mmmm……hard to tell when you don't really know someone. She went on, trying to sound casual and friendly.

"Yeah, pretty much the same in Boston this time of year actually. We do live in the same hemisphere you know." Terri didn't wait for Jonathan to comment on this. She figured she may as well 'cut to the chase' and see if he was in the mood to chat. "So, what's up with you? You missed a great dinner. Spaghetti, bread, salad, wine. I made the sauce myself. I'm sure we have leftovers if you haven't eaten." What had he been doing?, she wondered. It was nearly 9:00.

"Yeah, well I grabbed something downtown at the bowling alley. They've got pretty good burgers there. I'm not much of a family dinner guy." Jonathan certainly appeared uncomfortable but he made no attempt to get out of talking with Terri, so she moved on with her plan.

She put the book aside and got up from her chair. "How about we go outside for a walk? It's just *so* nice out." Not surprisingly, Jonathan followed Terri as she moved through the French doors, down the porch steps, across the lawn, and stepped out onto the pier. Geez, *men are so dumb*, she thought. At least men like Jonathan, anyway. They're like puppies or something the way they just follow you around. Not to mention their ridiculously huge, annoying egos. Like they think they're attractive to all women no matter what they look like or how obnoxious their personalities are. Not that Jonathan wasn't attractive. With his thick dark hair and sharp blue eyes, any girl would think him good-looking. Terri, at the moment, however, was trying to figure out what would trigger her cousin into trusting her.

Jonathan was close behind Terri as she walked to the end of the pier, *too* close for comfort but it wasn't as if he could do anything unseemly. There was a whole house full of people just a few feet away. She sat down on one of the benches and he sat next to her. "Anyway," Terri began, trying not to reveal how uncomfortable she was starting to feel, "what's up with you? You haven't been around much."

"What do you give a shit for?" Jonathan asked in a huffy tone. "It's not like we've seen each other in years. What are you, anyway? Some kind of a P.I., or something?"

Easy Terri, she said to herself. Jonathan was certainly agitated about something. It didn't take a private investigator to figure that one out. Make nice, she thought. "A private investigator, me? What, you mean like Magnum P.I. or something?" Terri laughed a little. "No, I'm just a humble caterer. My only business is food. You know, feeding other people has always been a pretty good business." Terri was *not* a caterer. Not by a long shot. She was much more than that. But she figured keeping it simple would be the easiest thing for her ditsy cousin to understand for now.

"Besides," she went on in a soothing voice, "you were the one that said we should get to know each other better. We are cousins, after all. Our mothers are sisters." To Terri's surprise, Jonathan laughed at this. But she ignored him and went on. She cleared her throat nervously figuring she may as well go for broke. "So.....what do you do with yourself all day, anyway? *You* know what I do. So what do *you* do?"

He laughed again and, to Terri's surprise, suddenly put his arm around her. "Never mind what I do. As soon as I get enough scratch together, I'm getting the hell out of here anyway. But I think you're right. We *should* get to know one another better." Then to her horror,

Jonathan leaned over as if he was going to kiss her. Terri, as she shoved him away with as much force as she could, quickly stood up to put some distance between them.

"Jonathan!" She yelled at him like he was a bratty little kid. "What is wrong with you? I don't know how they do things in Wisconsin but where I come from, *first cousins do not make out!*"

Jonathan stood up, too, and faced her. Terri realized then that he probably *was* stoned. She hadn't smelled anything on him but he could be using something other than just weed. The only thing between them now was her arm as she pushed him backwards. When he laughed again, she *knew* he was stoned and couldn't have been more blown away when he finally enlightened her.

"We *aren't* first cousins, you dork!" he said with another stupid laugh.

"What?" Terri was astounded. "What are you talking about?"

"We are not first cousins. We are not second cousins. Hell, we aren't even third cousins twice removed." Terri stared at him dumbfounded, as Jonathan continued.

"Oh, your *Uncle* Bill is my dad but Sue is *not* my mom. So, get the crystal clear picture? *We are not cousins.* So, how about it? Want to get to know each other better or not?" He pushed against her arm trying to get closer to her. Terri, however, with a much more determined and *stronger* push, proceeded, unceremoniously, to shove Jonathan right into the calm, clear waters of Green Bay!

Then, retaining as much of her dignity as she possibly could, to hide her total shock and surprise, Terri uttered but one word. "Not!" She then stormed to the house in search of her aunt, with her hands balled into fists, feeling again, like she wanted to punch someone. She could hear Jonathan splashing around in the water, swearing at her as she marched away. Now, who had the last laugh? Well, this *did* clear up something. Uh, sort of.

Chapter 13

Later, as they were getting ready for bed, Terri and Angie discussed the matter at great length.

"About the only thing this whole story explains," Terri said as she turned down the covers, "is why Jonathan actually thought in that pin-head, pea brain of his, that he could put the make on me. As far as I am concerned, we are still cousins and that is the end of it!"

Now *Angie* laughed. "So, what are you saying here? That you maybe *would be* attracted to Jonathan, or what? He is kind of cute but pretty damn screwed up. Can't say I'm interested in the guy myself. Now Zach on the other hand……."

Terri gave her a withering look. "Zach is too young for you, Ang. Besides, once we leave Wisconsin, it's bye-bye Robertson family." She waggled her fingers for effect.

Terri had been left no choice by Jonathan. She needed to find out what the story was from Aunt Susie. Everyone else was still in the basement or had gone off to bed. Terri found her mother and aunt in the study. Emily had been reading a book in a cozy chair by the fireplace in *that* room and Sue had been doing bookwork. When

Terri related what had happened, her Aunt Susie had sighed and looked as if she was ready to burst into tears.

"I'm so sorry, Aunt Susie," Terri said, hugging her aunt close. "But I think Jonathan is in some kind of trouble and I really was just trying to help."

"It's O.K., Terri," Sue had sniffed and grabbed a tissue. "I'm the one who's sorry and I will make sure Jonathan apologizes. He had no right to treat you that way."

Terri then suggested the three of them go to the kitchen for hot drinks. Once they were settled in the cozy breakfast nook with steaming mugs of creamy hot chocolate, Terri looked to her aunt. "You have to tell me the story, Aunt Susie. None of this makes any sense to me."

Sue looked at Emily and her sister nodded in agreement with Terri. "Time for it to come out, Sue. Let's at least tell Terri, anyway. It's not like the whole group has to hear the story."

Sue took a deep breath and a sip of her hot chocolate and began to tell the tale. When Jonathan had been six months old, his mother had run off with another man, leaving Bill and their baby son alone. "I will never understand how a mother can leave her child." Sue sipped her hot chocolate and sighed. "Jonathan was the most darling little guy I have ever seen. I fell in love with him, along with his dad, from the beginning. Bill and I met a couple of months after his first wife left. As soon as Bill could get an uncontested divorce, he and I got married. I raised Jonathan like he was my own son and we were always close. Pretty soon Courtney was born, then the twins, then Angelica. I always treated all of my kids the same. We didn't even tell Jonathan about his mother until he was twelve years old. We thought we could explain it, without making her sound like this horrible person, even though she was. Jonathan made up his mind, though, that he had to find her."

Sue stopped for a second to catch her breath before she went on. "Of course, your Uncle Bill objected. He had never gotten over Sara leaving him and their baby. That was her name. Sara. Bill never said a bad word about her in front of his son but somehow Jonathan knew anyway that it was a terrible story. He changed after that. You would have thought he would have been bitter toward me but he felt more angry with his father for some reason. I guess that *sort of* makes sense. He never stopped thinking of me as his mother. That was something, I suppose." Sue stopped at this point, like she couldn't go on. Emily and Terri waited. "You tell her the rest, Em," Sue said then. "I'm exhausted from this whole thing."

"O.K., Sweetie. Just try to relax." Emily took her sister's hand and gave it a tight squeeze. Terri looked expectantly at her mother.

"Jonathan *did* contact his biological mother. Young as he was, he was as sharp as a tack. He went around town, talking to people Bill had grown up with until he found someone who could tell him about Sara. When he finally found her, it turned out she was living in La Crosse. That's not that far from here. Well, unfortunately, when he went to see her, she rejected him completely."

"Oh no!" Terri said with dismay. "How can anyone act like that? Her own flesh and blood?"

"Oh, it gets worse," Emily said as she continued to comfort her sister. "Jonathan had gotten someone to take him to La Crosse to see her, of course, *without* Bill's permission. Sara told him straight out that she never wanted to see him again, *ever!* She was a total alcoholic and drug abuser." Terri could imagine what that must have been like, considering her experiences with Brianna's mother. This was not the time to bring that up, however. Emily went on.

"A few months later, word came to us that Sara had over-dosed and she was dead." Terri stifled another cry of dismay but tears sprang to her eyes.

"Oh, my God! What a horrible story. Oh, Aunt Susie, how did you ever manage that tragedy with Jonathan?" Terri felt terrible for her sweet aunt.

"We barely did," Sue said, her voice shaking. "Jonathan completely withdrew from us after that. 'If we had allowed him to see his mother sooner, she may have been saved,' he always accused Bill. But he was too young to realize that Sara had been abusing alcohol and drugs from the time he had been a baby. She drank heavily during her pregnancy and Bill had feared for the health of his child. Miraculously, Jonathan was born healthy. Bill had hoped that fact would help Sara to shape up but it was too late. As soon as the first guy came along, she took off and that was it. She was a train wreck waiting to happen. We also found out later that it hadn't been the first time she had over-dosed. *This time,* was the last. Seeing Jonathan really had just been too much for her, just as Bill had feared. But more than likely nothing could have saved her. God knows, enough people tried."

The story they had told her was so similar to what Brianna had been through with her mother, that Terri felt that strong sense of déjà vu again. Except Brianna's mother Elizabeth Severson, was still alive. Terri was ashamed to admit it but she wasn't so sure that was a good thing. Elizabeth had almost killed her and Terri would not forget how frightened she had been for a very long time to come. As a matter of fact, she was still afraid of Elizabeth. The possibility that the woman could come back into their lives in the future, absolutely terrified Terri. She said this much, as she relayed Jonathan's story to Angie, as best she could.

"Yeah, I don't blame you one bit for how you feel about Elizabeth. I think Brianna probably feels the same way. Geez, what is it with stupid people like that, anyway?" Angie gave a sniff of disgust. "It's like you can hand them happiness on a silver platter and they just throw it away with both hands. Elizabeth has certainly done that. She has had every opportunity to get her life together."

"Yeah, and now Jonathan is heading in the same direction," commented Terri. "Maybe his mother's drinking while she was pregnant with him, has affected his health after all. That would make sense, you know. Alcoholism can run in the family. He seems more interested in drugs, however, weed and stuff."

"So, what did Susie say when you said that Jonathan might be heading for trouble?" Angie slipped into bed and plopped down on her pillow with a heavy sigh. It had been another long, and slightly bizarre, day.

"Pretty much the same as Jonathan said, interestingly. Uncle Bill has been suspicious for awhile that he's up to something but they've gotten about as much out of him as I did tonight. Zip. Nada. They just have to wait and see what happens, I guess." Terri flopped down on her own comfy pillow and grabbed the soft pink teddy. Then she laughed. She couldn't help herself. "Man, Ang, you should have seen Jonathan's face when I pushed him into the bay. He is pissed at me!"

"Yeah, way to go. Can't say I blame you and I am truly sorry I missed it." Angie yawned and shut off her light.

Terri knew the conversation was done so she leaned over and switched off her lamp. Angie started breathing lightly and Terri knew she had drifted off. No one fell asleep faster then Angie. She was used to sleeping as much as she could, *when* she could. Vacation was no exception. Besides, they had a lot planned for tomorrow.

Terri, on the other hand, couldn't settle in as easily. After about 20 minutes, she got up and walked out onto their small balcony. She stared at the water for a few minutes, looking at the bench she had sat on with Jonathan. As her eyes adjusted to the dark, she picked out a small light in the general vicinity of the pier. Someone was out there smoking and as the smell drifted up to her room window, Terri realized that it was Jonathan. Smoking another joint, obviously, from the telltale scent. What was he thinking sitting out there, anyway? Terri had been sure he had left the B & B for the evening. The rest of the house was slumbering as it was nearly midnight, so he obviously felt safe sitting out on the pier alone. And what about the elaborate alarm system that was set at night by Danielle? Apparently, if Jonathan was on the property, he stayed in one of the apartments above the garage. She doubted he would reside in the main house where anyone could keep track of his comings and goings.

Did Uncle Bill realize that Jonathan smoked pot on a regular basis? Was it illegal in Wisconsin? Terri was pretty sure it was. Was he selling as well? Smoking it was one thing. Selling was a totally different situation. Tomorrow was Wednesday. Jonathan had mentioned something happening on Friday night, in his conversation with Franklin. Terri had *not* told Aunt Susie about what she had seen and heard on Cana Island, or about what she and Angie had heard in Jonathan's conversation on the phone with Franklin. She also had not mentioned his pot smoking habit. Her aunt had been pretty upset after having told Terri the awful story of Jonathan's biological mother.

Terri just couldn't bring up all the other complications in Jonathan's life at the moment. She and Angie had basically just stumbled onto all of it. They really didn't have anything to tell *anybody.*

What, exactly, was supposed to 'go down' on Friday night, as they say in the criminal or law enforcement world, depending upon which side you were on? Would it be possible to stop Jonathan from getting in any deeper than he already was? Did Terri even want to? If it meant making sure nothing happened to ruin Courtney's wedding, did she even have a choice?

Chapter 14

Thinking about Friday night, Terri realized there was nothing she could do about Jonathan. At least not at the moment. She had a rehearsal dinner to plan and as the maid of honor, to attend. After going over the details with Courtney, they came up with a count of an even dozen for dinner. Uncle Bill and Aunt Sue, Courtney and Jared, Jared's parents, Debra and Patrick, Terri and her escort, Jared's brother Mark, Danielle and Jared's college roommate, Tony, and finally, Angelica and Bryce, the young lawyer who worked with Jared in Milwaukee, were the twelve who rounded out the dinner party. Emily, Brianna, Zach, and Angie would expertly serve the meal. They would also enjoy their own share of the fabulous repast in the kitchen. The dinner itself was to be very formal and elegant with champagne and wines for each of the courses.

Terri was looking forward to the preparation and presentation of all the courses. Not only would it be enjoyable to do the planning and cooking but she really needed the learning experience. Especially working with the truffles. When Angie's step mom, Judith, had prepared a delicious dinner featuring truffles back in January, Terri had thoroughly enjoyed eating the fantastic meal. She had not been involved in the preparation, however. This time she would plan and prepare the courses, put the serving into the hands of her capable mother and friends, and then hopefully relax and enjoy the dinner.

The luscious steaming hot lobster tails, would be served with hot melted truffle butter drizzled over the baked tails, with extra butter in small cups on the side. Having decided on the appetizers, soup and salad, as well as the sides, to go with main course, Terri went to her favorite food and wine website for suggestions. She then chose appropriate wines to go with each course from Sue and Bill's wine cellar. Terri had been confident, from what she had seen, that there would be several very good selections to choose from and she was right. It had been difficult but fun, nevertheless, to decide which wines to serve. And since the rehearsal dinner was to be quite elegant, the wedding luncheon would be kept simple. Having the rehearsal dinner the week *before* the wedding had been Courtney's idea. The guests for the dinner would spend the weekend, head back to Milwaukee on Sunday, and then come back the next weekend for the wedding. Courtney and Jared would be going to Greece for their honeymoon. Sigh. If only, thought Terri.

In the meantime, they had some serious shopping and sightseeing to do. Courtney had appointments in Sturgeon Bay for most of the day. Danielle headed to her part-time job at the marina which would end with the tourist season. Terri, Angie, and Brianna, with Angelica driving her red Chevy Blazer, headed south down Hwy. 42 to Ephraim. There they split into pairs and walked through art galleries and shops before meeting at Wilson's to show off their purchases and have lunch. It was a charming spot, with a massive red and white striped awning coming off the roof and an outdoor patio with a screened-in porch. It was also a gorgeous day, so they opted for the outside tables and ordered delicious sandwiches and best of all, ice cream! Hot fudge sundaes were just the ticket and more good natured ribbing was aimed at Angie, as she once again moaned and groaned about gaining weight.

"That's it!" Angie said determinedly. "Tomorrow I am going for a hike. Man this is good stuff! Mmmm……..," she moaned again and they all laughed.

Over-Easy

"Fine, *take a hike,* if you want to Ang," Terri commented, as she dug into her own bowl, "but I have a big dinner to plan so no hike for me. Besides, I feel absolutely wonderful." Terri sighed and felt replete for at least a couple of hours anyway, until the next fantastic meal that is. "Huh, I wonder what Aunt Susie is planning for supper." She licked her spoon and pretended to think hard about it.

Angie narrowed her eyes at her friend and growled at her, making Terri kick her under the table. "Yeah, fine for you, Miss 'high metabolism.' You'll have to *roll* me back to Boston, I won't be able to fit into my uniform, then I'll get canned, and it will be *all your fault!*" She shook her spoon at her best friend as Brianna watched with amusement.

"Hey," said Terri, defending herself, "I'm not twisting your arm and forcing that spoon into your mouth!"

"They aren't really fighting, are they?" Angelica, momentarily concerned, asked Brianna in a low voice.

"Nay," said Brianna with a laugh. "Now watch Terri as she rolls her eyes and completely ignores Angie and….."

"O.K., stop that!" Terri finished the last of the chocolate in the bottom of her sundae glass and wiped her mouth with a napkin. "Angie may have me here, though. Suddenly, I feel stuffed."

"You're not gonna hurl again, are you?" Angie pretended to be concerned and got an 'if looks could kill' shot from her best friend.

"Again?" Angelica was mystified. "Ooooo……I smell a story. Give it up, Cousin."

"Yeah," Angie said mischievously, "give it up, Cousin!"

Terri looked around at the expectant faces and suddenly said, "Time to go!" Angelica dived for the check but Brianna was too fast for her as the party broke up.

"Aw, c'mon," Angelica complained, "just when it was getting interesting. And Brianna, I have never seen anyone grab the check faster than you!"

Brianna countered by sticking out her tongue and waving the check in front of Angelica's face as Terri's frustrated cousin tried to grab it. Brianna whipped out her credit card and fairly danced to the cash register with Angelica following helplessly.

"Children, please! Behave yourselves." Terri scolded the two younger girls. "Everyone in here will think we're all a bunch of nuts!"

"Trust me, Terri," said Angelica nonchalantly, "nobody cares." Terri looked around at the other patrons in the charming restaurant. Angelica was right. Nobody did care. Ah, to be that relaxed all of the time, she thought. Now that's a real vacation!

"Don't we have more shopping to do, anyway?" Angie asked cheerfully. "What's the next town down? Um, Shark Creek or something?"

"Ah....yeah, that would be *Fish* Creek," corrected Angelica. "We don't have sharks here. This is Wisconsin, remember? Not the coast of Maine."

"Du-du.........du-du…..du-du-du-du-du-du-du-du-duuuuu!" Angie did her best to pull off the music from 'Jaws' and everybody laughed. Interesting how that theme was so universal. Mr. Spielberg had truly created a monster. Terri was glad there were no sharks in Wisconsin, that was for sure.

Also, hoping that the subject had been changed, Terri pinched Angie, who pretended exaggerated pain as they all piled back into the Blazer.

"No, I mean *really*," Angelica said, not wanting to let it go. "When did you hurl and what's the drama behind it? Mmmm...... suddenly, I don't just smell a *story*. I smell a *man*!"

Feeling a little ruffled under the circumstances, Terri tried to laugh it off. "Maybe I'll tell you sometime but you'll have to get me drunk first."

Brianna snorted at this and Angie scoffed. "Yeah, like that'll ever happen. Terri *never* gets drunk, Angelica. Forget it. Not only is this saga on going though, it *has* reached a critical point."

Angelica looked confused as she glanced at Brianna. "Straight ahead," Brianna directed, pointing south. Then she whispered to Angelica, "I'll tell you later."

"I heard that!" Terri said from the backseat. In the meantime, she decided to let it drop and thought over her most important purchase so far. She had found a gorgeous print of the Cana Island Lighthouse and intended to hang it behind the cash register in their store back in Boston. The island seemed so mysterious to her. She just couldn't put her finger on it. She longed to go back there but there were just too many other things to do. More importantly, however, Jonathan was up to something with his buddy Franklin and Terri was just itching to get there Friday night and see what was going on. But she had no idea what time they were meeting and the dinner would go on until about 8:30. Also, by that time, they would have all consumed several glasses of different wines, not to mention cocktails before dinner, to go with all of the fabulous food. Going anywhere would more than likely be impossible. And they would all be exhausted, especially Terri.

The most important thing to Terri, however, was to make sure the best was gotten out of the extravagant meal with the main course not being served too late. It was bad for the digestion to eat late in the evening, especially when one is indulging in such rich foods. Terri, for herself, was very strict about this rule. Good thing she had gotten out of the restaurant business when she did. Large meals going out of the kitchen, often as late as 10:00 or 10:30 in the evening, had made Terri sick to her stomach just watching it. Oh well, there was a night life in *every* big city and sometimes it meant eating late. But staying up all night partying and then sleeping all day was not for the working class. It certainly wasn't for Terri or Angie, not since college anyway. They both loved their jobs. So that meant staying on a healthy schedule of meals and rest. But for now, they were on vacation.

As they reached Fish Creek and drove past the school, the road twisted and turned, moving down a rather steep hill toward the downtown. There were many shops and small eateries along the way. Angelica made her way through a 3-way stop, drove down one block, and making a right turn, parked on a side street where several shops were located on both sides of the street. Up the hill, to their left, was Founders Square which, of course, consisted of yet more clothing stores and gift shops.

"What time you guys want to meet back here?" Angelica asked looking at her phone. "It's about 1:00." Angelica's phone made a musical sound as she was looking at it and she jumped in surprise. "Geez...." she shrieked. "Oh, it's Mom." They talked for a few minutes and Angelica asked for a piece of paper. "O.K., Mom," she said laughing, "now I gotta make a list!" Terri pulled a small note pad and pen out of her purse and handed them to Angelica.

"We'll meet you guys back here at 2:30. How does that sound?" Terri asked Brianna. Brianna nodded as Angelica was busy jotting down a list for her mother, so Angie and Terri dodged into the nearest shop. It was called Vagabond Imports and was packed with all sorts of 'groovy' things. A hippie guy at the cash register greeted them as they started looking at bags and colorful shirts. "I wonder if my dad would wear something like this." Terri took an outrageously wild button-down shirt off of a rack and Angie laughed. "What do ya' think?" She held the shirt up for her friend's perusal.

"Maybe," Angie said. But then she turned serious. "You know, Terri, you gotta tell Brianna what's going on and *soon*. She's been looking at you like your face has suddenly turned green."

"Yeah, I know, and it probably has," said Terri, not the least bit disturbed by Angie's suggestion or her earlier teasing, for that matter. It was no secret that Terri had been dating a police chief back in Boston. She would have some explaining to do pretty soon one way or another, especially to Brianna.

"She knows me too well." Terri sighed, as she continued to look through colorful shirts and warm sweatshirts. "Even my mom didn't figure out that something was wrong, until she eavesdropped on us that is. I can tell Brianna knows something is up. Besides, Rico hasn't called me so, obviously, there is a problem. Pete has certainly kept in contact with *his* girlfriend enough. That hasn't helped my situation any."

Pete Fazio was Brianna's boyfriend and they all liked him very much. He was *extremely* Italian and lots of fun with gorgeous thick black hair and huge happy brown eyes. And even though Brianna was only nineteen years old and Pete a mere twenty, they already seemed destined to be together forever. Brianna had met him at school and said she felt like she had known him all her life. Terri agreed. He was an awesome find in an uncertain world and gave Brianna the security she had been looking for all of her life. Especially, since he a had a huge Italian family, complete with a welcoming mama, Rosa, who loved Brianna like she was her own. Of course, Rosa, also cooked fantastic Italian meals, like nothing *even Terri* had ever tasted in her life. Pete also had three sisters and two brothers, giving Brianna the large family she had always longed for, with lots of fun siblings to love. Terri, Angie, Rico, and Will had already been welcomed into the Fazio home for several delicious Italian feasts, just as if they, too, were long lost family.

Terri had yet to even *meet* any of Rico's relatives, which was another thing that had bugged her for a long time. And it would have been just one *more* thing to bring up the last night she had seen him. She was glad now that she hadn't. It would have only meant more disappointment for her.

Terri sighed again with the same frustration she always felt when she thought about Rico these days, and decided, what the hell?, as she chose a shirt for her dad. Terri knew he'd wear it just because she had picked it out for him. He was always looking for something different or goofy to wear when he went fishing or clamming with his buddies. They would all get a kick out of it. Especially when Harvey told them his daughter had bought it for him in Wisconsin. Terri also chose three pairs of soft, tight-fitting gloves, two black and one gray, for a mere $5.00 a pair. And she couldn't believe it when she found a coffee mug with her favorite work of art in the whole world painted on it.

"The Scream?" Angie, as always, was flabbergasted by her friend's taste in great works of art. "You gotta be kiddin' me! Have you *seen* those movies?"

"Oh, c'mon," protested Terri, "those movies are just plain dumb. Although, the first one was kind of brilliant. Mmmm......anyway, this particular work," she patted the coffee mug for emphasis, "has always fascinated me. No one really knows what emotion Munch was painting when he did this. *Why* is she screaming? That's the big question." Terri paid for her purchases and the hippie guy at the cash register agreed.

"Jamie," he called waving at them, "c'mon, lunchtime!"

"We're coming, Michael," Jamie called back. Then turning once more to Terri she said, "Have a wonderful day and enjoy this gorgeous weather."

Suddenly forgetting how badly she needed to use the bathroom, Terri watched the young mother join her husband and older daughter. What an adorable couple, she thought. They appeared to be perhaps in their middle twenties, nicely dressed, and happy. But the face of that little girl was implanted in Terri's mind. Little Hailey looked over her mother's shoulder and waved at Terri, wiggling the tiny fingers with the thumb still in her mouth. Terri waved back and couldn't help but think how much her own mother would adore a grandchild like that! Grandchildren for her mother and children for herself, seemed more out of reach than ever now. Terri felt a painful lurch in her stomach. Maybe *that* was Rico's problem. Maybe he didn't like kids. But that couldn't be it. He had been wonderful with Jenni and Benjamin and she knew he had nieces and nephews. He had spoken fondly of them many times.

Oh, and how simple life was when you were small and innocent. And Terri had never seen a more innocent, yet somehow wise, face then little Hailey and doubted she ever would again.

She ducked into the bathroom, finally remembering *exactly* why she was standing there. She stayed in the small room for quite awhile just to ponder and feel sorry for herself. She thought about Jonathan and how it must have made him feel when he realized his own mother had left him and hadn't wanted anything to do with him. *And Brianna.* How hard it had been on her, the way her mother had treated her more like a possession than a daughter. The contrast between what Brianna and Jonathan had been through with their mothers, seemed all the more sad as Terri thought about little Hailey and the love her mother and father obviously had for her and her big sister. It was so easy to recognize genuine love over the selfish kind that destroyed people, killed their spirit, and inevitably ruined their lives.

Finally, realizing she couldn't stay in the tiny bathroom all day, Terri moved to open the door and heard people talking outside.

Cigarette smoke drifted towards her but when she heard *who* was talking, she stifled her reaction and didn't move. *Jonathan again!* What the hell was going on here? Terri was starting to feel like she was going completely bonkers! Well, at least he wasn't taking drags out of a joint right in the middle of Fish Creek!

"Regan, please," Jonathan suddenly sounded like he was begging for his very life, "you have got to stop this *stupid* plan of yours. This is the worst idea in the *history* of worst ideas, *ever!* You can't decide to get rid of someone just because you're sick of hearing them complain. Besides, Franklin isn't that bad. And *I do not* want to be involved with this! I *can not* be involved with cold hearted murder!"

"Shut the hell up, Jonathan, and keep your stupid voice down!" Regan commanded sharply. "You are such an idiot, and I am *sick to death* of Franklin Stone!" Terri controlled a sharp gasp at this revelation. "He is nothing but a pain in the ass. Every time I talk to him, he makes *more* threats and expects to get *more* money. I don't trust him and it will be soooooooo…..easy to make it look like an accident. Besides, he's old anyway, *nobody* likes him, and I doubt that anyone will miss him! Now stop being such a damn stupid wimp and do what I tell you to do, before something happens to *you!*"

Terri had to force herself to control the wave of nausea that suddenly came over her, obviously *not* just from the cigarette smoke. She waited another couple of minutes and hearing no more voices, finally opened the door. No one was around. She quickly high-tailed it out of the small restroom, thankful no one else had come along to use it. Being the middle of the week in the fall of the year, there weren't as many tourists in the area. Which was probably why Regan and Jonathan didn't think there would be anyone around to hear their conversation. Well, they were dead wrong. Angie would not believe this!

Terri saw her friend waiting on the bench outside of Pelletier's and ran toward her. Angie looked up and saw Terri and was just about to yell at her when she caught the look on her friend's face. "Terri, what's wrong? You certainly were in the bathroom long enough. Are you O.K.?" Angie grabbed Terri's shoulders and saw the alarm in her friend's eyes. "What's happened? What?"

Terri grabbed Angie by her elbows to steady herself and started to explain, keeping her *own* voice low. "Angie, you won't believe this." Terri felt panic setting in. This was too much. Talk about being in the wrong place at the wrong time, or was it the right place at the wrong time, or.....

"Hey, guys!" They heard Brianna's voice, temporarily interrupting Terri's explanation. She looked at Angie, giving her a sign her friend knew well. *Wait for it.*

Brianna took one look at Terri and knew something had happened but chose wisely not to mention her concern in front of Angelica. "Um, yeah, we're going that way." Brianna pointed towards the downtown area. "Angelica said there's some neat shops down there. Where are you guys headed?"

Angie spoke up to give Terri a minute to collect herself and looking over her shoulder, saw a clothing shop called 'Weber's.' "Yeah, we'll try that one," Angie laughed nervously. "Susie told Terri and I that we had better get some more, 'regional' outerwear. Ya' know, something besides Red Sox tee shirts. Stuff that says Door County on it, I suppose." She pushed Terri in that general direction and they parted ways from the two younger girls once more. Angelica had assured them they would definitely find what they were looking for in that particular shop.

Instead of going in the shop straight away, however, they found another bench to sit on away from any buildings. Terri was terrified someone might hear *them* talking. Angie, being the good police officer she was, understood completely. After Terri told her what she had overheard, Angie was as dumbfounded as her friend.

"O.K.," Angie said, trying to remain calm, "what have we got here?"

"Um, um, I know!" Terri said a little too enthusiastically. "When we were trying to figure out what had happened to Logan, Guerrero told me to put everything down in a computer file and then keep track of....."

Angie impatiently cut off her panicky friend.

"Well, yeah, great idea old buddy, but we don't have a computer at our disposal at the moment. Just let me think, O.K.?" Terri nodded. "And for Pete's sake Terri, try to calm down. You look like a maniac!"

Terri *felt* like a maniac. What would they do if anything happened to Jonathan? How had Ed Stone's brother, obviously Franklin Stone, ended up in Door County, Wisconsin? Wasn't he supposed to have died a long time ago? Cal had always said that Ed had a brother who had died years ago but he had never mentioned a first name. Had Ed and Franklin had some kind of a falling out and never spoken again?

"Uh, shopping!" Angie said then, as if she was having a revelation.

"What?" Terri felt completely disoriented.

"We have to *shop*, dodo," Angie dragged her friend by the hand towards Weber's. "We have to shop for clothes and stuff, *right now*! There is nothing else we can do at the moment and we are wasting time. If we don't buy anything, it's going to look really strange. C'mon, Terri, snap out of it!"

Angie was right so they proceeded to shop with abandon. They bought Door County t-shirts and sweatshirts in several different sizes and colors for everybody back in Boston. They also chose more coffee cups and mugs, sofa pillows, and random jewelry. By the time they came out of the shop, they could barely carry what they had purchased, but the sales people at Weber's were *very* happy.

"O.K., well this looks pretty nuts, that's for sure," Terri said, completely loaded down with bags and packages. Then, looking in the direction Brianna and Angelica had gone, they saw the two younger girls coming toward them, equally weighted down with shopping bags. Terri actually laughed, although she did sound slightly hysterical. "Oh good. Look at those two," she said with relief. "Maybe we don't look so goofy after all."

"Yeah, and good thing too," agreed Angie. "I think we've done enough shopping for today." Then before they reached the other two girls, she whispered to Terri. "I also think the first thing we need to find out is, who is this *Regan?*" Terri agreed.

Unknown to Terri and Angie at the moment, however, they would soon find out *exactly* who Regan was. And, as it turned out, they didn't have very far to look.

Chapter 15

Dinner that night turned out to be casual. The next evening would be the fish boil, and then the elaborate rehearsal dinner on Friday night. So for this Wednesday evening, the kitchen was open with leftovers, sandwiches, or whatever each person could come up with on their own. Some opted for leftover spaghetti. There were also plenty of sliced deli meats with good breads, fresh fruits, and cheeses, always kept on hand at the B & B. Terri, after having a glass of White Zinfandel to calm herself down, quickly put together a small cheese, meat, and fruit tray for everyone to munch on, along with a bread and cracker basket. Then, finding several boxes of beautiful fresh mushrooms in the walk-in, Terri proceeded to make a large pot of a soothing and delicious mushroom and rice soup, to go with the sandwiches and cheeses. She needed to do something with her hands so she could relax and being a cool evening, it was perfect for soup. They all enjoyed it and Aunt Susie asked for the recipe.

Terri and Angie needed to talk with Brianna and bring her 'up to speed' on what was happening, as soon as possible. If they were going to get themselves involved in an actual investigation, they might as well engage Brianna as a backup. The girls also realized that they really had nothing solid to go to the local police with. They had no idea who Regan was, no idea what part of the community Franklin Stone was involved in, and couldn't risk Jonathan getting into anymore trouble than he already was. Terri would probably just end up painting herself as some kind of a loony. Not to mention the fact that she was a tourist. From what she had surmised, like any tourist area, Door County loved the vacation people. *But* they were also very protective of their own. Terri and Angie had no business accusing anyone when they had so little to go on. So far, they had no *real* evidence of anything, aside from what they had heard and no real proof to back up any criminal activity. People said stupid things all of the time and local authorities were normally unable to react until an actual crime had been committed. It happened all the time. People's lives seemed to be in danger, then nothing occurred. Unfortunately, only too often, things *did* happen, terrible things, to people who had been threatened. But for now, Terri and Angie were helpless. It was a very bizarre set of nothing but circumstantial evidence and that was sketchy at best. All they could do was wait.

As it turned out, Brianna agreed with Terri and Angie. After they had finished eating, the three of them had gone to Terri and Angie's room to fill Brianna in on all the details. Terri sat cross-legged on her bed holding the soft pink Teddy bear for security. Angie plumped up her pillows to lean back on and Brianna pulled up the rocking chair with the big Raggedy Ann doll on her lap. After Terri and Angie had related all of the details and weird happenings of the last three days, Brianna got up from the rocking chair. She plopped Raggedy Ann down at the foot of Terri's bed, and began to pace back and forth, mulling it all over before she commented.

"Sooooo….., let me get this straight," Brianna began. "Terri, you and Rico have broken up, which is why you have been so sad and depressed since we left for this trip. And yeah, no matter how hard you have tried to cover it up, I noticed right away and just waited for you to tell me." Terri didn't doubt her. Brianna went on. "So then, Terri, the *very* first day we are here, you saw a young guy and some older man named Franklin, who looked an *awful* lot like Ed Stone, arguing on Cana Island when you went for your walk after lunch." Terri nodded but remained silent.

Brianna continued. "*Then,* that very evening, Jonathan came to the house after the barbecue outside. You were down on the pier and, hearing Jonathan speak, you figured out he was the young guy on Cana Island. Rather than deal with meeting him at that point, you snuck into the house. That was Monday. So, we get to Tuesday. *Both* of you hear Jonathan talking on the phone to Franklin. He mentions in his conversation on the phone with Franklin about something happening on what you assume is Cana Island, Friday night. Then he lights up a joint and takes off." Angie and Terri nodded again and Brianna paced a little more before she went on.

"So......then *Tuesday* night, Jonathan tried to hit on you, Terri, and revealed that you are *not* actually cousins. You then proceeded to push him into the bay. I would have loved to have seen that, by the way." Terri made a face, Angie nodded and laughed, and Brianna went on. "So you immediately go to your Aunt Susie and she tells you the very sad tale of Jonathan's birth mother. So, Jonathan wasn't giving you a line of bullshit. You *are not* cousins. What a dork, though." Terri nodded.

Brianna paced a little more. "Then today, Terri, you just *happen* to be in a small bathroom in Fish Creek where you overhear yet *another* conversation, this time between Jonathan and someone named Regan. Jonathan begs this Regan person, not to go through with a possible plan, to, *get rid of,* " here Brianna used the *dreaded* finger quotes for emphasis, "Franklin Stone. Hearing the last name Stone, you assume that Franklin is more than likely Ed Stone's long lost brother. Have I covered everything?" She looked at the other two women expectantly.

"I.......think so," Terri said. She felt almost like a little kid being questioned by her mother. She also never failed to be surprised at how mature and practical Brianna was.

"Yeah, sounds like you covered everything," Angie confirmed.

"All this and we've only been here for three days?" Now Brianna was dumbfounded.

"Correct," said Terri. Angie just nodded.

"Unbelievable!" Brianna grabbed Raggedy Ann, plopped back down in the rocker, and gave the poor doll a tight squeeze. But as it turned out, Brianna had important information of her own that would totally blow Angie and Terri away. She went on with her ruminations.

"O.K., you two," Brianna began, but suddenly, she looked like the cat that had swallowed the canary. "First of all, Terri, do not *ever* keep anything from me 'cause you think I will freak out or be upset, or whatever. *Yes*, I miss my grandfather terribly and Ed Stone was a total bastard. *Yes*, my mother is a complete psycho and I'm managing to deal with it, better than you would think. But I've learned a lot from what I've been through with my mother and from Ed Stone's murder, *and* from the loss of my grandfather. So I can pretty much handle anything, thank you very much. So don't hold stuff back from me again, *ever*. Agreed?"

Terri nodded and said apologetically, "Agreed. I swear, no more secrets." She held up two fingers. "Scout's honor."

Angie looked at her and made a goofy face. "You've never been a girl scout. That was me, remember? That's why I became a cop. Or that was at least one of the reasons anyway." Terri's young business partner ignored this as she went on.

"O.K., then." Brianna paused a bit at this point for just a little more affect. "Well, here's the best part of what *I* have to tell *you* guys. And who would have thought that *I*," she placed a hand importantly on her chest for emphasis, "would have something to add to this already *very* complicated story? I mean, since up to this point, I haven't really even been involved." She was enjoying the suspense just a little too much.

"You wanna tell us what the hell you're talking about?" Angie was losing patience by now. "The suspense is killing me!" Brianna smiled and finally came out with her dramatic announcement.

"I know who Regan is," she revealed to her friends, grinning smugly as she paused for their reaction.

"What? How could you possibly? We haven't even had a chance to....." Terri thought she couldn't be surprised anymore. At least not today anyway. She and Angie looked shocked as Brianna went on.

"Well, Angelica was talking about the fish boil at Pelletier's tomorrow night and you know how Courtney said that her friend works there?" Terri and Angie nodded. "Well that *friend* is Regan! Angelica just happened to mention her name while we were shopping. Not exactly a name you hear everyday of the week, wouldn't you agree?"

"Good work, Brianna!" said Terri, clapping her hands and hopping off of her bed to hug her brilliant young assistant.

"Well, thank you, Boss," Brianna beamed, "but it really took so little effort on my part. Glad that I could be of assistance though."

"Holy shit!" was Angie's comment as she fell back on the pillows, hitting her head on the wall. "Ow!" she said then, rubbing her noggin. Terri and Brianna laughed.

Suddenly Terri felt better. *A lot* better. Now they had Brianna to help. The *three* of them, together, could figure this out.

"All for one?" Brianna said, putting up her hand.

"And one for all!" Terri and Angie said as they smacked their palms together.

"Suddenly, I feel like watching 'The Three Musketeers,'" said Angie, with a relieved laugh. "A little Kiefer Sutherland and Charlie Sheen anyone?"

"I'm game," said Brianna, hopping up and moving the rocking chair, along with Raggedy Ann, back to its corner.

A movie was just what they needed. Brianna went in search of Angelica and Danielle. Angie took off to see about refreshments.

"Hey," Terri called after them, "how do you know they even *have* 'The Three Musketeers'?"

Angie stuck her head back in the room and simply said, "I brought my copy. Are you comin'? We're on vacation, remember?" Then she disappeared again.

Terri, however, had a lot of work to do in the next couple of days. Snacks and a movie would be a perfect way to relax while she still could. And *maybe* another glass of that delicious White Zin would be in order. Definitely, *maybe*.

Chapter 16

Terri had just one day, Thursday, to pull together the details for the elaborate rehearsal dinner, with Friday to prepare it. She had checked supplies and surmised that anything else needed could easily be found, if not in Aunt Susie's amazing pantry, somewhere in Sister Bay. The beautiful lobster tails were thawing in the walk-in refrigerator. The truffles had been carefully removed from their tightly sealed packages and the *aroma* was permeating everything. A truffle shaver had been packed in the boxes with the food by the girls back in Boston. Terri had selected several wonderful cheeses and the appropriate crackers on which to serve the caviar at a store in the Country Walk Shops in Sister Bay.

Also, just in time, Brianna's father had sent a whole case of a fabulous, *rather expensive,* champagne, with a note which read: To the Happy Couple! Hope you are all having a wonderful time. Kind Regards, David Severson. Terri was pleased as the champagne would go perfectly with the caviar and other appetizers. Courtney was delighted and understandably surprised.

"Wow, Brianna and her father certainly are generous," she commented as they examined the beautiful bottles. "I had better send this guy a *really* nice thank you note." Terri agreed. You have no idea, she thought but wasn't about to enlighten her cousin. Even Emily didn't know just exactly how wealthy Brianna and her father were.

But more importantly, and much to Terri's relief, she and Angie now had a comrade in Brianna who would keep her eyes and ears open for anything else suspicious. They certainly had plenty to go on but little to report to authorities. Brianna's sudden disclosure of who Regan was really had come as a complete shock to her friends. And no one had seen Jonathan since Terri had heard his conversation with Regan in Fish Creek, *also* much to Terri's relief. She had enough on her mind the way it was, without another weird confrontation with her screwed up, 'not her cousin,' cousin. This would certainly be a weird story to explain to her sisters and brother. Rachel and Beck would be arriving next Thursday. Danielle and Emily would be driving to Milwaukee to pick them up. Her brother, Rob, could hear the bizarre tale another time.

In the meantime, Terri was forced to make the decision that there was no way she would be able to attend the fish boil.

"I have *got* to stay here and get everything ready for this dinner," she explained to Angie and Brianna. "You guys go to the fish boil, see what *our dragon lady* looks like, and note anything strange. Better yet, just note anything at all."

With apologies to Courtney and her aunt at breakfast on Thursday morning, it was also agreed that Danielle would stay behind to help Terri.

"I've been to my share of fish boils," said Danielle to Emily and her mother. "It will be an honor to stay here and help Terri plan the rehearsal dinner. Besides, I can really use the experience."

Thursday turned out to be another gorgeous day. Angie, Brianna, and Angelica headed up to Northport at the tip of the peninsula for the hike Angie wanted, to walk off all of the fabulous food and drink they had already indulged in. Susie had prepared smoked turkey and ham sandwiches for their lunch. Along with plenty of bottles of cold water and fresh fruit, she had packed everything into backpacks and the girls had cheerfully gone on their way.

Terri and Danielle proceeded to choose appropriate stemware and silver serving pieces, as well as plan the arrangements for the table settings. Apparently, Aunt Susie had several sets of china up in the third floor attic. Terri and Danielle would choose from one of them. They would also look over what was on hand for formal table cloths with matching napkins, as well as napkin rings. Sue had already come up with pretty place cards for each setting on which Danielle had carefully spelled out the name of each guest in beautiful calligraphy lettering. Just another hidden talent of Terri's amazing cousin. This dinner was shaping up to be fabulous and gorgeous, as well as delicious.

"How did you get the names on so perfectly?" Terri admired the place cards as they looked over silver pieces and sparkling wine glasses.

"Trial and error, my dear cousin, trial and error," said Danielle. "It would be impossible to get the names on perfect free hand. You just outline the size of the card on a regular piece of paper and practice putting in the letters. Taking the number of letters in the names and measuring carefully from each end, you figure out how much room you will have according to the number of letters. And it can get pretty tricky when you're putting Courtney one card and Mark on another. There's nothing worse than getting to the end of the card and not having room for a T or something." Terri laughed.

"Yeah, and you don't want to waste these," she said, holding the pretty cards and examining the beautiful lettering. "It's nice to have 'em too, so we can decide where everyone is going to sit."

In the meantime, guests for the dinner party were beginning to arrive. Even the short drive from Milwaukee to Door County could be exhausting. Jared and his parents arrived at the B & B on Thursday afternoon. They too would be attending the fish boil at Pelletier's. Jared's brother, Mark, along with his groomsmen, Bryce and Tony, were all meeting in Milwaukee on Friday morning and driving up to Sister Bay. They would arrive in the afternoon, an hour or two before cocktails for the rehearsal dinner.

Over-Easy

Terri was relieved to finally meet Jared and his parents and she liked them all immediately. They were casual, attractive, and easy-going.

"I have been hearing about this amazing rehearsal dinner we will be having, from Courtney," said Jared's mother, Debra. "I have been *so* looking forward to it, Terri, and to meeting you, your mother, and your friends. I know it's going to be a wonderful week." Debra and Joseph would be staying at the B & B for the week until the wedding. Jared would drive back to Milwaukee and then come back next Friday.

Debra gave Terri a warm hug as if they had been friends for a long time and Terri appreciated her kind words. Jared's mother was also about the same age as Emily and Sue so the older women had lots to talk about. Jared's father, Joseph, was a hometown boy who had lived in Wisconsin all of his life. He reminded Terri of her own father, as in, not exactly a formal dinner and wedding, kind of guy but he would deal with it for his son. More than anything, Joseph wanted to go fishing with Bill. They would go on Saturday, Bill had promised. Accommodations had been arranged for everyone. Debra and Joseph had a bedroom upstairs. Zach was on hand to settle Jared into one of the apartments above the huge 3-car garage. Mark, Bryce, and Tony would also bunk in the *guys* apartments, as Terri had come to think of the living quarters above the garage.

And then there was Jared. He was perfect for Courtney. Terri could see how much they had in common. They pretty much finished each other's sentences. Terri always took that as a good sign with a couple. Had she and Rico ever done that? Weird, but all of a sudden, she could barely remember him. It was like she had been in this other world of Door County forever. It had been less than a week since she and Rico had argued after their last date. Now it just seemed fuzzy and surreal to her.

Jared, on the other hand, was the complete opposite of Rico. He had light, almost blonde, soft thick hair with pretty blue eyes and eyelashes way too long for a man but they somehow suited him. He and Courtney almost looked like brother and sister, another strange phenomenon Terri had noted over the years in couples who complimented one another. Jared always had a protective arm lightly around his fiancee when they were together but not *too* protective. Just enough to show how much he cared for her and that he was just happy and content to be with her. He was slim and just a couple of inches taller than Courtney. They were absolutely lovely together.

Terri had good feelings about this marriage. In this day and age, when half of the marriages in the U.S. ended in divorce, it was one of the most difficult steps to take for a couple, to be sure. Terri, however, still *wanted* to be married. She wanted that family she had been thinking about and suddenly, she still wanted it to be with Rico. How though? Could she maybe call him and try to mend the fences? Was it even up to her? If the other person didn't care about you, they didn't care about you. That was it. You couldn't *make* someone love you. How would she know how he really felt if she didn't talk to him? They would need to have it out sometime to settle things one way or another. Anything further than that these days, was just plain called *stalking*. A sensible person had to know when to back off and then simply move on.

But then she remembered her own words. "I'm in love with you, Rico….I want to get married and have a family. What's *your* problem?" Terri recalled the look of dismay on his face. What *was* his problem? When she got back to Boston, she would have to deal with it. She would have to deal with Rico. She couldn't stay in Sister Bay forever. It was like a make-believe world. She didn't want to stay here forever, though. She needed to go back to her life in Boston. Back to her business, her friends, her fuzzy kitties, not to mention her faithful employees and customers, who were depending on her, along with Kelli and Amber.

Terri was interrupted from her thoughts as her mother spoke to her from what seemed like a far away place. "Terri, honey," Emily laid a hand lightly on her daughter's arm, "we want to put together a quick lunch for Jared and his parents. Could you help me while the others are visiting?"

Terri shook herself as if she had the chills and Emily looked at her with concern. "Sure, Mom," she said with a smile, much to Emily's relief. They moved to the kitchen where Terri's mother quickly cut

Over-Easy

to the chase. They had very few chances to be alone on this vacation so if they were going to talk, now was the time.

"What's on your mind, Sweetie?" Emily opened the huge fridge and started taking out meats and cheeses. Terri quickly grabbed a large round silver tray, covered it with clear plastic wrap, and began to arrange the food in an attractive, as well as appetizing fashion.

"Well," Terri wasn't sure where to begin, "I guess I'm having kind of a difficult time dealing with this wedding all of a sudden. That dopey Rico, I just want to strangle the guy. I...." Terri wasn't sure *how* she felt anymore. Certainly, she wasn't jealous of her cousin. "I really am happy for Courtney and Jared though, Mom. They are perfect for one another."

"It's O.K., dear. I know you are happy for Courtney," said Emily, understanding completely. Then after a short pause, she dared to ask the question that had been on Terri's mind. "I don't suppose you could just give the dope in question a call?"

Terri laughed without amusement. "Weird," she said to her mother, "I had just been thinking that exact same thing myself. But I don't think so." She sighed. "You didn't see the look on his face when I told him I was in love with him, Mom. He was completely thrown for a loop." Emily nodded and waited for further explanation. "It was like the whole idea had come totally out of left field for him. I mean, what the hell did he expect from me? I guess I just expected too much from him maybe, huh?"

"No, I don't think so," Emily said wisely but she tried to carefully ponder every word she said to her daughter. The last thing she wanted was for Terri to feel like her mother was interfering. "I've watched Rico when you haven't. He looked perfectly comfortable with our family. It seemed like he fit right in, like he wanted to be there." Emily paused and took out bags of green and red grapes, along with a box of luscious red strawberries from the fridge. Terri carefully rinsed the fruit and placed it on clean towels to drain.

"Yeah, I have to go along with you on that, Mom." Emily was again relieved by her daughter's response. "I guess that's why I kind of figured he was the one." Terri shrugged and sighed again. But then she had a thought that made her feel like she shouldn't give up after all. "Mom," she said in a voice that made Emily perk up with hope, "I'm not at all sure what is going on with Rico but I do know this. I intend to find out. I'm not going to just let him go. Whatever he's been through, it can't be so terrible that he...." But that was as far as Terri got. Courtney flew into the room as if she was being pursued by angry bees.

"Terri," she was both happy and anxious at the same time, "how's lunch coming? Oh, man, can you believe it? I'm getting married in like, a week? You guys like Jared, right? Aren't his parents nice?" Courtney started going on and on. Emily and Terri smiled at each other and quickly reassured the nervous bride. A few minutes later, the group sat down to a simple lunch of fruit, deli meats, breads, crackers, and more delicious Wisconsin cheeses. Terri made a fresh pitcher of lemonade for the women as Bill and Joseph enjoyed cold bottles of Miller Lite, also in true Wisconsin style.

Terri made herself scarce after a few minutes and went in search of Angie and Brianna. Then, remembering they had gone on a hike up to the tip of the peninsula, she retired to her room for a few minutes alone. She felt oddly comforted by her talk with her mother. Funny, she thought, if my mom had tried to talk to me about my love life ten years ago, I would have had a conniption. Now, I just feel so much better. I must be finally growing up. That too, was a comforting thought, and soon she found herself drifting off. Afternoon naps were getting to be a bad habit, Terri thought, as she fell asleep. They would be few and far between once she got back to work and everyday life in Boston, however. Might as well enjoy it while she could.

Chapter 17

Terri opened her eyes and was startled to see Angie in the other bed slumbering peacefully. How long had she been asleep? Was it night time?

Definitely not. The sun was still shining. Terri grabbed her phone and saw that it was about 3:30. Angie, Brianna, and Angelica must have gotten back from their hike. Terri couldn't believe she hadn't been disturbed when Angie came into their room. I must have been sleeping like a stone, she thought, as she quietly got out of bed and went into the bathroom. She splashed some water on her face and ran her fingers through her hair. She still looked tired. Tired and sad. I have got to cheer up, she thought. This was a vacation, despite all the work that needed to be done. Work she also knew she would very much enjoy.

There was still a lot to do for the rehearsal dinner. She had kind of abandoned Danielle. They hadn't even finished choosing all of the serving pieces or made a decision on which china they would use, since they had been interrupted by the arrival of Jared and his parents. Terri then felt her stomach growling. She had actually *forgotten* to eat lunch in favor of a nap. Emily, Sue, and Bill had been

"Yes, Jonathan?" Terri looked around the refrigerator door and saw that her aunt was shaking her head.

"Um, ah...."

"You said that already," Terri pointed out.

"Um, I really *am sorry* for the way I treated you," Jonathan was making the ultimate effort. "I was a jerk. O.K? So, I admit it. Are you guys happy?"

"A *wasted* jerk?" Terri also added.

"Yeah. A stupid, idiotic, moronic, *wasted* jerk!" Jonathan took a breath and looked down at his untouched plate. Terri could tell it was killing him, so she decided to stop the torture treatment. Men! Heaven forbid they take responsibility for any mistake.

"O.K."

"What?" Jonathan looked at her with big eyes, still in shock.

"I said, O.K. That's the end of it." Terri made herself a turkey and Swiss cheese sandwich with wheat bread and a wonderful honey mustard. She also grabbed a fresh bottle of water, along with a napkin, and then looked at her cousin pointedly. "I don't bother myself using up my precious time and energy being pissed off at people for any sizable length of time. So, it's done. But...."

"Uh-oh. Here it comes!" Jonathan said with disgust.

"Yeah, uh-oh," Terri said. "Here's the thing, pal. You are my *cousin*, get it? Nothing more and, certainly, *nothing* less. I don't care what your story is or if you are wasted or not. If you *ever* try to pull anything like that on me again, I will gladly, and with absolutely no remorse, break your arm. Got that?"

"You can do that?" Jonathan looked astounded.

"Yeah, I can do that. Do *not* underestimate me. I can do a lot of things. At this point, you would be much better off to have me on your side. Are we agreed?" Terri stuck out her hand. Jonathan took it and firmly shook hands with her.

"We are agreed." He also appeared petrified.

"Well, I'm certainly satisfied," said Aunt Susie, with obvious appreciation. "I've also got other things to do. Jonathan, eat your ham and eggs," she said simply and left the kitchen.

Terri, with sandwich, water, and napkin in hand, did the same and headed upstairs to talk to Angie before the group left for the fish boil. Terri assumed she had left her *cousin Jonathan*, with a lot to think about. Mission accomplished.

When she got back to their room, Angie was just waking up. Coming out of a stupor was more like it, though, from the way she looked.

Terri took a bite out of her sandwich and waited for her friend to come around. "What's the matter with you?" Terri asked as Angie groaned.

"'Take a hike,' she said. 'Work off the calories,' she said. Oh, God, I'm gonna die!" Angie fell back onto the pillow with a thud and pulled the covers over her head.

Terri laughed, this time however, with *genuine* amusement. Taunting Jonathan had given her an extreme adrenaline rush. Teasing Angie was almost as much fun.

"Get up, you wuss!" Terri poked at what she figured was Angie's head.

"You've got spying to do. This is no time to wimp out!"

"No!" Angie's voice was muffled under the blankets. "I want to sleep for about two days. Leave me the hell alone!"

"Take a shower. You'll feel better. My grandma always says that." Terri took a bite out of her sandwich and a long plug from her water bottle. She then proceeded to pull the covers off of her grousing friend.

"Damn it!" Angie yelled. Despite her protests, however, she slowly got up, grumbling all the way, made her way to the bathroom, and in a few seconds, Terri heard the shower running.

Terri went to the small balcony and looked out at Green Bay. The leaves were just starting to turn and there was a perfect breeze blowing the trees and bushes back and forth. Small waves were moving in the bay and they washed pleasantly up on the sandy beach and pier. It was very picturesque and calming. Terri took a deep breath of the lovely fresh air and tried to focus on the days ahead.

Despite her apparent victory over Jonathan, there were still so many questions. Questions she dare not ask, at least not for now, especially in front of her aunt. If Terri seemed even a *little* too interested in just exactly what line of work he and Franklin were involved in, she would lose her edge over he wayward *cousin*. He would know she knew something was going on and quickly clam up. Obviously, the fact that he had admitted being wasted, or whatever the proper term was, hadn't been any kind of an issue or surprise to her helpless aunt. Sue had probably given up ages ago trying to control, or at the very least, help, her son. And he was *her* child. Terri could see that now. The relationship between Jonathan and Sue appeared to be genuinely affectionate and stable. Definitely better than anything he would have had to go through with his birth mother. Brianna was a living, breathing example of that. Emily had welcomed Terri's young friend into a circle of genuine love and protection and Brianna basked in the warmth of the close Springe family. Blood wasn't *always* thicker than water. Sometimes, it meant nothing at all.

Angie came out of the bathroom, still moaning and groaning, interrupting Terri's musings. She sat on the edge of her bed in a comfy blue robe and proceeded to slowly towel dry her hair. But she appeared as if she was doing a little better.

"That must have been some hike," Terri commented as she threw her napkin into a small waste basket and sat down on her own bed across from Angie. "You think you feel lousy now, wait until tomorrow. Ha!" Terri laughed again. She suddenly felt giddy with power.

"Oh, thanks a lot for that old buddy," Angie said, but she did sound better. "I guess that's what I get for not going to the gym more often. Who has time for that anyway? There must be *some* fit people out there! Anytime I *do* go, the place is packed!"

"Yeah, well forget about all of that for now," Terri showed no mercy. They had other things to contend with. "You have to be sharp for tonight."

Terri then related her conversation with Jonathan to Angie, perking her friend right up, as it turned out. Sore muscles forgotten, she listened carefully, and when Terri finished, Angie let out a low whistle.

"Wow," she said. "So Franklin and Jonathan, and apparently the mysterious Regan, must have some kind of a business going to cover what they're *really* up to. You think?"

"That's certainly a possibility. But what? Yard work? Painting? Roofing? There's all kinds of different things people hire out these days. My mom cleaned houses for twelve years while she was raising us kids. Somehow I can not picture Jonathan scrubbing toilets, though. How are we going to find out?" Now Terri was feeling frustrated again. Wasted or not, she dared not ask Jonathan anymore questions. For now, they needed to be on peaceable terms.

"I don't know," said Angie, as she ruffled through her clothes to pick out a suitable outfit for the fish boil. "All we can do is wait and see, I guess. We aren't going to be here that long, ya' know, so this mystery may not get solved while we are even here." Terri looked suddenly deflated and Angie had to laugh this time.

"Hey, cheer up! At least no one has tripped over a dead body yet. That's something." Angie pulled a Boston Red Sox t-shirt over her head and had such a naughty look on her face that Terri fell back on her bed with a case of unstoppable giggles.

"Oh, Ang," she said, "I can't believe you! All those Door County shirts we bought and you're right back to the same old stuff you'd wear to a Sox game back home. What will Aunt Susie say?" She laughed some more.

"Oh, I don't know. That I look like a tourist?" Angie put her hands out in a ta da, motion and Terri just shook her head. But then she got serious.

"Well, whatever you're wearing, just remember, you're on a mission. Got that, O-O-7?" Terri raised an eyebrow at her friend.

"Got it, Sherlock! I just hope that I can at least enjoy the food," Angie lamented.

"After that hike? You deserve it," Terri countered. "Just don't miss anything. You're right. We don't have much time. We better make the best out of what we have left." Angie saw the look on best friend's face. She was determined. Angie could understand that. Terri didn't want Courtney's wedding ruined. They also felt like Jonathan might be in real trouble, maybe even in real danger. Discussing actually 'getting rid of' someone, was not exactly the kind of talk to be taken lightly. In the meantime, all Angie could do was go to the fish boil, keep her eyes open, along with Brianna, and whatever happened, try to keep Terri from getting into trouble herself. These days, that was getting to be no easy task.

But Terri had one more thing to add, much to Angie's dismay. "Oh, and by the way, *do not drink any alcohol!* You need to completely keep your wits about you, got that?"

"Great," Angie groused, "so much for having fun at the fish boil."

"You can have fun without drinking," Terri said firmly, shaking a finger at her friend. Then realizing she sounded like a prudish old lady, she added one last thing. "Just keep your ears open and your eyes peeled."

"Yes, Mother," Angie said, rolling her eyes. Terri just shook her head and sighed. Sometimes she really *did* feel like everyone's mother!

Chapter 18

Terri and Danielle finally decided on a beautiful set of china for the rehearsal dinner from several choices stored in the huge attic that covered the top of the whole house. The dinnerware looked delicate but was really quite serviceable as well as beautiful. Tiny perfect pink roses with bright green and gold, stems and leaves, edged the dinner plates and coffee cups, and decorated the centers of the smaller pieces. Taking the boxes carefully down the steep stairs and to the kitchen for Terri and Danielle to examine and clean, had been exhausting, so they had stopped for a break. Danielle was having a glass of the fresh lemonade that Terri had replenished and Terri was sipping a bottle of ice cold water, her favorite beverage.

"You sure drink a lot of water, Terri," Danielle remarked. "I would imagine that helps you maintain your weight. They say you should drink, what, like eight to ten glasses of water a day?"

"Something like that. My mom is the same way," Terri said. "She's been carrying a cell phone and a bottle of water for as long as I can remember. Now everyone is doing it."

"You know, that's weird. You're right about that," Danielle said. "Mmmm…..anyway, so we've chosen the china. Now what about the eating utensils?"

"Oh man, we don't have to go to the attic again, do we?" Terri groaned.

"Nay, most of the silverware is in the china hutch," Danielle laughed. "I'm sure we'll find something appropriate. But you can't even imagine what is in that attic. It's like another house up there!"

"Yeah, I saw that," Terri finished her water and placed the empty bottle in the recycle bin by the washers and dryers. "We'll save that tour for another day. Let's get all the dishes and stuff taken care of and then I have to see what else can be done tonight."

With the china, silver pieces, and crystal glassware all chosen, Terri went through the menu for like the twentieth time and was satisfied with all of the courses. Now, as long as the timing was kept in check, everything would be perfect. Whew!

Terri then showed Danielle how to prepare the lobster tails for baking. The beautiful large tails had all arrived frozen solid and were now arranged on a big flat tray to thaw. Terri pulled the tray out of the walk-in fridge and placed it on the counter. Taking the first thawed tail in her left hand and a kitchen shears in her right, Terri cut down the middle of the back of the shell to the bottom of the tail. Danielle followed suit, cutting the tough shell of the lobster she was holding.

"O.K.," Danielle said as she cut carefully through the back of the shell, "this isn't as easy as it looks."

"No, it's not," Terri agreed, "but after you've done like a thousand of them, you get the hang of it. We used to have to do dozens in one day at Twin Pines when there would be parties for like, two hundred people. Sometimes I would go home and I couldn't feel my fingers." Danielle shook her head.

"The restaurant business is not for the faint-hearted, that's for sure," Terri said, "but I wouldn't have missed it for the world. I learned so many things about food and how to prepare a lobster tail for cooking, was just one of the many."

Once the shell was cut as far down the back as possible, Terri carefully pulled the lobster meat out of the shell and placed it back on the tray. Taking the meat out, without removing it from the shell, she placed the meat on top of the empty shell, fanning it out evenly over the top of the closed shell beneath it. Splashed with lemon juice and white wine, then baked in a 375 degree oven until firm, white, and no longer translucent, the cooked meat would rest on top of the shell. Then brushed with hot melted truffle butter, sprinkled with bright red paprika, and garnished with fresh parsley for a lovely presentation, they would be colorful and beautiful on the plate. With more hot truffle butter and fresh slices of lemon on the side, they would *taste* fabulous.

"I can't wait to dig into these," said Danielle, as they finished preparing all of the lobster tails for cooking. "Providing I still have an appetite by the time we get to them," she added. "You have so many wonderful courses planned, Terri. I hope we aren't all full by the time we get to the main event."

"As long as the timing is carefully followed, there shouldn't be a problem," said Terri as they washed their hands thoroughly after handling the raw seafood. "This dinner should take *at least* three and half hours, leaving plenty of time in between courses to rest our tummies."

"That sounds good. So we've got *just* the tails here. Have you ever prepared live lobsters?" Danielle shivered just thinking about it.

"Are you kiddin'? I'm from Boston, remembaʼ? And yeah, loads of ʻem. I really do prefah to work with just the tails myself. But there's nothing like a fresh lobstaʼ right off the boat for *good* eatin.'" Danielle laughed at Terri's exaggerated Boston vernacular as they dried their hands and started to carefully put china plates, saucers, cups, and silverware into the dishwasher. As soon as all of the pieces were sparkling clean, dry, and carefully examined for any cracks or chips, the girls placed them on clean towels on the counter.

"Amazing," said Terri as she examined a beautiful dinner plate, "every piece, in perfect condition! Not one tiny little chip on any of them. At least none that I can see. Your mom has taken really good care of these dishes. They are just gorgeous."

"Yes, they are," agreed Danielle, "but you want to hear the scariest part? My mom has *at least* another half dozen sets up in the attic that are probably just as nice and just as beautiful. She is a terrible pack rat. We need to have a huge garage sale one of these days!" She laughed as she put down a delicate coffee cup.

"I suppose you could do that," Terri said. "But make sure you give me first dibs. 'Course, then I'd have to get them back home without incident. Damn, there's always a catch. Huh."

"Well, then, it's a good thing we didn't look at all of the other sets," Danielle observed. "You would have never been able to make up your mind and chose just one!"

"Yeah, we would have run out of time by now," Terri agreed. "There are so many details when you're putting together a dinner like this."

Hearing voices from the front of the house, the girls stopped what they were doing and left the kitchen. "Wow, I can't believe it's that late already," Terri said as her mother and Sue came through the dining room. "How was the fish boil?" Terri asked as she gave her mother a hug.

"Wonderful," Emily gushed. "You really missed it! It was fun and the food was fabulous. What did you girls get done?"

"Come to the kitchen and see," Terri said as she noticed Angie and Brianna coming in behind them, followed by Angelica. Uh oh, thought Terri, when she saw Brianna. Her young business partner had that, *'she looks like she's seen a ghost,'* expression on her face. Terri guessed that Franklin Stone had made an appearance at the fish boil. These days, as Brianna herself had pointed out, it took a lot to get to her. And apparently, something finally had. But they wouldn't even be able to discuss it until later. The rest of the group was starting to come into the B & B. Jared's parents were also very pleased with the evening, but tired. Aunt Susie and Uncle Bill brought up the rear of the group. Jared and Courtney had gone for a drive, it being such a beautiful evening. Uncle Bill looked beat but convinced Jared's dad, Joseph, to head to the basement for a night cap and maybe a quick game of pool. Bill had been surrounded by women for most of the

Over-Easy

week. He was enjoying finally having another guy around to hang out with. Danielle said she was tired and headed off to bed.

Sue, Emily, and Angelica admired the dishes. "Oh, Terri," said Sue, extremely pleased, "I'm so glad you chose these. This is one of my favorite sets. Aren't they gorgeous, Em?" Emily picked up a dinner plate and also fussed over the silverware and crystal.

Terri shook her head and smiled at her mother and aunt. Sheesh, old people are so funny, she thought. Suddenly, though, she got a signal from Angie. Taking a closer look at Brianna, she knew they needed to talk and *right now!*

"I'm glad you're pleased, Aunt Susie," Terri said, hugging her aunt and kissing her cheek. "They will be perfect. Ah, say Angie, why don't we go up to our room and you can tell me all about the fish boil?" Now there was a lame excuse, if she ever heard one.

Terri was relieved to see her mother and aunt still examining the dishes and glassware and not paying attention to the girls. "I'll come with you." Brianna said, sounding edgy, which made Terri immediately alert. What the hell had happened?

"Hey, Bri," Angelica called after her, "wanna' watch a movie or something? You're not ready to call it a night already, are you?"

"Yeah, I'll be back down in a few minutes, Angelica," Brianna tried to sound casual. "Terri and I need to talk about the business a little, K?" Terri, Angie, and Brianna quickly headed upstairs, leaving a confused Angelica behind.

Closing the door as Brianna and Angie went into the bedroom ahead of her, Terri turned around to question her two friends. "What the hell happened at that fish boil? Brianna, you look like you're ready to freak out or something!" Brianna sat on Terri's pink bed, drawing her legs up under her and hugging the soft pink Teddy bear, looking like she was ready to cry.

"Yeah, well, didn't *you* feel the same way after *you* saw Franklin Stone?" Angie defended Brianna's reaction.

"Yes, yeah, I guess I did," Terri admitted. "I didn't want to believe what I saw." She sat on the bed with Brianna and took her hands. "Bri, what happened? Tell me what you're feeling."

"I guess not," Angie said simply. "I saw her right away 'cause I was right next to her. A couple of the wait staff quickly came over to clean up the mess, so it probably wasn't a big deal for them. But there was so much noise and activity going on, I just got her out of there as fast as I could and no one else noticed what had happened." She shrugged but then raised her eyebrows as she saw Terri looking behind her. Angie turned around. The door to their bedroom was slowly opening.

"I noticed," said Angelica, as she stepped into the room and *firmly* shut the door. "Want to fill me in on what's going on? Oh, and by the way, you guys have just gained another partner."

Chapter 19

"Oh crap!" said Angie, as Angelica plopped onto the foot of her bed. "So, how long have you been listening?"

"Long enough," Angelica admitted. "The door was *not* completely closed. That one kind of sticks sometimes. I just stood there and listened. Just like in the soap operas."

Terri just grinned and rolled her eyes, not the least bit surprised by Angelica's sudden entrance. The three of them had been acting pretty weird when they ran upstairs. Brianna suddenly perked up at the appearance of Angelica, however, and looked as pleased as punch. She liked Angelica. She liked her *very* much. "Guess I'm not the only one listening behind doors these days," Terri said, shaking her head. She could have sworn that she had closed that door.

"Yes!" Brianna said excitedly, as tears and fright forgotten, she grabbed Angelica in a convulsive hug. "I think she can be very useful to us, Boss." She looked at Terri for approval and got a laugh out of Angie.

"Hey, you don't have to sell me on my own cousin," Terri reminded her. "We can always use another opinion, not to mention an extra look-out. O.K. then, fine. Also, if need be, now we can split into pairs. Let's see if we can fill in the blanks for you, Angelica."

"Hey, this has got to better than any movie we could watch," Angelica was excited. "Oh, and I do love a good intrigue!"

"Oh, brother," Terri said, and then started the story with what she had seen *and heard* on Cana Island the very first day of their vacation. By the time they finished filling her in on all the details up to that point, it was nearly midnight and everyone was yawning.

"So, Angelica," Terri wanted to remind her of what they would need for her to do, "think about everything we've told you and try to remember if you've noticed anything strange about Jonathan lately."

"Uh, Terri, Jonathan always acts strange," Angelica reminded her cousin.

"O.K., fine then," Terri couldn't argue with that, "stranger than usual. Also, see what you can find out and tell us about Franklin Stone. What kind of business are they involved in? That kind of thing." Angelica had to admit that she hadn't a clue.

"I haven't paid a lot of attention to Jonathan in the last few years," she had to confess. "As a matter of fact, though, he has been hanging around home more than usual these days. And yeah, we all know he smokes pot. That's not a secret so I hope he's not fooling himself into thinking that he's hiding it or anything. He's already gotten a couple of tickets. I don't know why he hasn't learned anything when he gets caught. What a dork my brother is, anyway."

"So, did you know all along then, that your mom wasn't Jonathan's biological mother?" Angie wanted to know.

"Actually, no. We all found out just a few years ago. It came out when Jonathan had a bad reaction to penicillin. Ya' know, mold. Neither my mom or my dad ever had that problem. It's not that uncommon I guess but turns out that Sara, Jonathan's real mom, did. Dad let it slip out and well, the rest, as they say, is history." Angelica shrugged.

"Well, for tonight, so am I," Terri stretched and yawned. "If we don't all get some sleep right now, that fancy dinner that is supposed to go off tomorrow, or rather," she looked at the clock that said 12:30, "later today, will never happen."

Angelica and Brianna finally said goodnight and headed for their rooms in the huge basement. Terri took the bathroom first and was practically comatose by the time Angie came out after her turn and fell into bed.

"Holy man," said Angie. "I'm not sure how much more excitement I can take on this trip. You can't even imagine the look on Brianna's face when she looked across that fire and saw Franklin Stone standing there. I thought she was going to go completely nuts on me. I couldn't get her out of there fast enough."

"Shit," said Terri, upset with herself. "I should have been there. That poor girl. I know exactly how she feels. Well, maybe not *exactly*. I didn't have to put up with that creepy Ed Stone hanging around my house while I was growing up. Then all that horrible stuff comes out about him and her mom. Brianna is blowing me away with how she's handling it all though. This would be too much for me. She is an amazing girl. Don't you think, Angie? Angie?" But Angie was sound asleep, of course. Tired as she was, Terri *never* went to sleep as fast as her friend.

"Unbelievable," Terri said to the darkness as she stared up at the top of her canopy bed and hugged the pink Teddy bear. "I've just got to get through this dinner tomorrow night. What *else* is gonna happen before this is all over?"

Chapter 20

Terri was doing one last check on the appetizers to be served with cocktails and the champagne. She glanced at the clock. 4:30. The cocktail hour would began at exactly 5:00. She had just enough time to get dressed. Her hair and nails were done. All she needed to do was put on her make-up and the skirt and blouse she had chosen for the dinner. Mark, Jared's brother and Terri's dinner partner, as well as the best man for the wedding, was very nice and quite good looking. He was also engaged, *very* engaged. Not that it mattered much to Terri. His fiancee would be coming back with him next week-end for the wedding. Terri couldn't help but wonder how *she* would feel if she was engaged to Rico and he went to a nice dinner party to which she was not invited. Probably just a tad bit put out. Although, what could be done, when an occasion and dinner of this magnitude was so limited? From what she understood, all of the groomsmen had girlfriends. A dinner party for twelve could not be adjusted to accommodate everyone's love interests.

Terri sighed. She had actually made the horrible mistake of calling Rico's cell phone about an hour ago. She just wanted so badly to try to make peace with him, to hear his voice. He had not answered his phone, however. Terri wasn't sure which was worse. If he *had* answered and they had gotten involved in an awful argument, that would have solved nothing. It would have only made her evening miserable. Yet she pictured him looking at his phone, seeing it was her, and deliberately *not* answering it.

Terri drew in a shaky breath as she looked at the appetizers. The ones that needed to be heated, rested on trays ready to be slipped into the oven. The caviar was on ice, as well as the champagne. Two trays of the lovely Wisconsin cheeses, cubed, sliced, or in triangle shapes, were arranged with fresh fruits, along with the fabulous pate de foi gras. Terri suddenly realized she was famished and was just about ready to spread some of the pate on a cracker when she was startled by someone else coming into the kitchen.

"Hey, caught you!" Angie said as she saw Terri poised over the pate with a spreading knife.

"Just one," Terri said with a smile as she spread the lovely mixture on a buttery, crisp cracker. "Mmmm......" she closed her eyes and savored. "This is ambrosia." Angie followed suit and made corresponding yummy noises.

"Hey, girl," Angie said then, "shouldn't you be getting dressed?" Then she looked at her friend. "What did you do? Did something happen while I wasn't watching you?" Angie really was concerned. "Yummy pate or not, you *do not* look happy."

"Oh, yeah," Terri confessed, wrinkling her nose and filching another cracker. "I did a really dumb-ass thing. I tried to call Rico."

Angie was not about to scold her heartsick friend. "I don't think that's dumb-assed at all," she said, and then cautiously went on. "So…….. what did he say then?"

"Um, nothing," Terri backed out of the walk-in fridge and firmly closed the door.

"Nothing." Angie was confused.

Terri looked at her pointedly. "He did *not* answer the phone."

"Oh," Angie didn't know what to say. But then she realized what Terri was thinking. "Hey, Terri, c'mon now. There could be any number of reasons why he didn't answer his phone. Don't let it ruin your whole evening by imagining the worst."

"It's a little hard *not* to imagine the worst, I'm afraid," Terri said. "But I will not let it ruin my evening. I promise you that." Then steering away from the subject, she surmised her friend up and down. "*You* look very professional, by the way. Like a real waiter in the sharpest eating establishment, *ever*." She adjusted Angie's bow tie and picked a piece of lint off of her shoulder.

"Well, yeah, I feel like a penguin," Angie said, running a finger along the collar of her shirt. Terri laughed and felt better right away. Leave it to Angie to cheer her up.

Brianna then entered the kitchen dressed in the same fashion as Angie. Along with Emily and Zack, they all wore crisp white shirts, black vests, black bow ties, and black pants, all supplied by the B & B that were kept on hand for catering purposes. "Terri," Brianna sounded scandalized, "what are you doing in here? Get upstairs right now and finish getting ready!"

"O.K., I'm going, I'm going," Terri said. "You don't have to get so pushy."

"Terri," Brianna put her hands on her boss's shoulders and looked her straight in the eyes, "please, please, just relax and get the most out of this wonderful evening. Angie, Emily, Zach, and I will make sure everything is perfect, alright? I *do not* want to see you back in this kitchen tonight. Is that clear?"

"Crystal clear," Terri agreed solemnly. "Thanks, you guys. I don't know what I would do without you. O.K. then, here we go."

Chapter 21

An hour later, Terri was sipping the fabulous champagne and surmising the evening thus far. Soft classical music from the stereo in the background was playing just loud enough to go with the low hum of pleasant conversation among the guests. Courtney looked wonderful, of course, happy and relaxed in a royal blue flared skirt and creamy silk blouse. Her beautiful engagement ring sparkled as she gestured and laughed. Terri had chosen her favorite skirt, a straight, deep cranberry red pencil skirt that came just below her knees. With it, she wore a short-sleeved soft black, knit V-neck sweater, topped off with a simple gold chain and gold earrings in the shape of hearts.

Along with the cocktails, everyone was gushing over caviar and cheeses. For hot appetizers, Angie had talked Terri into serving the asparagus bites with truffle oil that Judith had made for the dinner she had prepared for them back in January. They were so fabulous, Angie had said, she couldn't get enough of them. Of course, they had needed to call Judith for the recipe which she had promptly e-mailed to them. Thank goodness for modern technology. They were also enjoying deviled eggs, with truffles, of course. And for a second hot appetizer, one of Terri's specialties, savory stuffed mushrooms, were also being served. Large white caps were filled with a delicious mixture of shrimp, fresh bread crumbs, thinly sliced green onions, and spices.

With the appetizers, they were enjoying the delicious champagne that had arrived from David Severson. An Italian sparkling wine, it was a 1993 Ca'del Bosco Cuv'ee Annamaria Clementi. Terri had guesstimated that the wonderful bubbly was probably, *at least*, $150.00 a bottle. Very generous indeed. They had chilled four bottles for the dinner. The rest would be served at the wedding reception. When asked about the champagne, Courtney had said only that it was a gift, not revealing, upon Terri's request, who the fabulous gift was from.

Not all were drinking champagne, however, as some of the men were having mixed drinks. Zach was behind the small bar in the corner of the living room area serving up the liquid refreshments. He would also help Emily plate up the dinners in the kitchen. Angie and Brianna would serve the guests at the table.

Terri, in the meantime, was having a difficult time concentrating on the conversation she was engaged in with Jared's mother, Debra. Between fuming about Rico not answering his phone, to wondering what was going to be going on over at Cana Island later, Terri had all she could do to be polite, at the very least. Debra didn't seem to notice, however, as she went on and on about how much she loved Door County. Terri strained to answer yes or no in the appropriate places. She was relieved however, when, right on schedule, Brianna came in to announce that the dinner guests were to move to the dining room for the soup course.

Everyone exclaimed over the beautiful dining room and the table, set with the lovely china, sparkling glassware, and lovely flower arrangements. Even the men were appropriately impressed. Bright pink candles were lit on the table and wall sconces surrounding the room. Pink and white roses with baby's breath and greens were set into arrangements at each end of the table. A large bright pink candle in the middle of the table finished off the decorations. Everyone looked for their name on the pretty place cards to see where they were to sit.

Joseph, the father of the groom, sat on one end with his wife Debra, to his right. Bill sat on the other end with Sue to his right. Next to Sue was Mark, then Terri and Courtney, with Jared next to his bride. On the other side of the table, Danielle sat next to Debra, with Tony, Jared's college roommate, next to her. Angelica and Bryce, the young lawyer in Mark's law firm, rounded out the table.

Before them were steaming bowls of chestnut and sherry soup with truffle garnish. Crystal water glasses were filled and bread baskets were placed on both ends of the table. Terri had decided not to serve wine with the soup course, to give the guests time to let the champagne and before dinner cocktails settle a bit. A good rule of thumb for any dinner party is to make plenty of water available to the diners, to help settle their stomachs, clear the palate, *and* the head. Along with warm, soft homemade dinner rolls, spread with whipped truffle butter, they all savored every last drop of the delicious soup. Terri was very pleased with how it turned out.

As Brianna and Angie removed the soup bowls and plates, conversation turned to the weather. *Especially* in Wisconsin, did conversation always turn to the weather as it was ever-changing, anytime of the year. They had a saying here in Wisconsin that was used often. 'You don't like the weather here? Wait five minutes!' That was certainly true. But so far on their vacation, the weather had been wonderful. A thunderstorm was predicted for the week-end, however, and Terri was looking forward to it. It would be awesome to watch the storm over the waters of Green Bay.

"I think I can see the leaves just starting to change," Debra remarked. "It should be beautiful for the wedding. Will you bring in most of your flowers for the winter, Sue? I normally take in just the potted ones." Yes, Sue answered back, most of the pots were stored in the basement for winter, especially the ones in the gazebo. The men talked about baseball. No Milwaukee Brewers or Boston Red Sox in the play-offs this year, however.

"The Brewers have some good young players," Bill said. "Time to turn things around and make Miller Park worth all the money they put into it. We hope to get down there next year for some more games. Only made it to one this year. Pretty busy summer."

Terri and Angie were missing several Red Sox games while they were gone but the series was not in the grasp of Boston, this year. So being away wasn't such a big deal. Terri stayed out of the baseball talk, however. With everything that had been going on, she hadn't even had time to miss her beloved Red Sox. There had been way too many distractions.

Salad was next. Terri had also decided to keep this simple. Fresh, crisp mixed greens of romaine, iceberg, and arugula, with freshly snipped herbs, and thin radish slices, tossed with a dressing of balsamic vinegar and extra virgin olive oil, was placed before them. Water glasses were replenished, ice cold and clear with brightly shining cubes, clinking musically onto crystal. Everything looked so beautiful in the candle light. With the salad, a 2004 Ecco Domani, Pinot Grigio, Delle Venezle was poured. Chilled, crisp, and citrusy, it was delicious with the fresh greens.

Terri was feeling a bit giddy from her triumph of the dinner. It was but half over though, so she tried to relax and look calm, even though she was feeling anything but. She took another sip of wine as Brianna and Angie began to remove the salad plates.

"Did everyone enjoy their soup and salads?" Brianna asked as they all made positive comments. "The best is yet to come. If you would all like to relax, stretch your legs, or whatever, we will be serving the main course in about 20 minutes." It was always a good idea to take a bathroom break, especially with all the wine being served. Terri found herself standing on shaky legs, however, as got up from her chair.

"Whoa," said Mark, grabbing her elbow, "you O.K., Terri?"

"Yes, Mark, thank you," Terri gave him a friendly smile. "I'm fine. This is quite the finish to another long day. I might be getting a little tired." Mark was the perfect gentleman. Terri couldn't deny that. Probably missing his fiancee though, she thought wistfully, as she headed for the nearest restroom. Not forgetting her promise to stay away from the kitchen, she headed to a small bathroom next to Aunt Susie's study.

Emerging from said bathroom about 10 minutes later, Terri noticed car headlights coming into the driveway. Obviously, everyone staying at the bed and breakfast was already in the house. So when Terri saw Jonathan get out of his rather beat-up old Ford Taurus, she felt nervous and dismayed. What would they do if he was drunk or high and crashed this dinner party? Should she go find her Uncle Bill and ask him to speak to Jonathan before a problem arose? Would Aunt Susie be a better choice to handle him?

Terri watched Jonathan anxiously. He seemed to be steady on his feet as he looked toward the house. But then, understanding dawned on him. A family party he certainly had not been invited to. Terri saw the hurt look on his face and suddenly felt a little sorry for him. His apparent sobriety may or may not, have forced him to make the right decision, however. After only a moment of hesitation, he jumped back into his car and carefully backed out of the driveway. Terri had to admit she was grateful to Jonathan for not making a scene, or even throwing a hissy fit by making as much noise as possible as he took his leave. He left quietly and politely and Terri was proud of him. Maybe they would have a chance to talk about things and settle it before she went home to Boston. But where was he going now? To the Sister Bay Bowl for a sandwich, maybe? Perhaps he had friends he could hang out with. And then later, would he go to Cana Island to meet Franklin and the mysterious, possibly even dangerous, Regan?

"Terri," Brianna was suddenly at her side and Terri nearly jumped out of her skin. "What are you doing? It's time to serve the main course."

"Oh, Brianna, I'm sorry." Terri felt ashamed of her bad manners. "I'll tell you later, O.K? I……." But Brianna was behind her boss, pushing her back to the dining room. There would be time for explanations *after* this dinner. Everyone else was seated at the table waiting for her.

"Terri," Courtney said, sounding a little nervous, "you almost missed your own grand finale." Courtney looked at her disoriented cousin as if to say, 'What is wrong with you'? Terri sat down carefully and squeezed her cousin's hand to reassure her.

"Excuse me, everyone," Terri smiled at the rest of the guests. "I didn't mean to get distracted. Let's proceed, shall we?" Brianna was standing by the kitchen door looking professional and expectant. Terri gave her a slight nod to proceed.

Brianna disappeared into the kitchen and then quickly came back out with Angie right behind her. Starting with Joseph, the father of the groom, they placed warm plates in front of the diners that were beautiful to behold. Luscious, perfectly cooked lobster tails, pristine white meat brushed with truffle butter, sprinkled with bright red paprika and freshly snipped parsley leaves, were placed before them. Also, on the plate with the lobster, was yet another one of Terri's specialties. Twice baked russet potatoes, also brushed with truffle butter and served with whipped sour cream. Added to the plate, were crisp green beans, tossed with sweet onions and thin slices of fresh carrot, to finish off the main course. Everyone applauded and congratulated Terri's planning of the dinner as Brianna and Angie proceeded to pour the wine.

Terri had chosen a red *and* a white, to go with the main course. Each diner was given a choice of which they preferred and it was poured into the appropriate wine glass. The white was a 2004 Chateau Bonnet, Entre-Deux-Mers, another citrusy choice. Her other choice was a 2002 Chateau Bonnet "Reserve" Bordeaux, an earthy red, with dark berry fruit flavors.

Terri was pleased to see the wine divided up nicely among the twelve diners. Just enough in the glass to sip but not too much, which could ruin a good meal. The lobster was tender and sweet, the potatoes and vegetables, delicious, and the perfect compliments. The meal was so fabulous, Terri was almost sorry it was nearly over. Her initial nervousness had finally disappeared. Her relief when Jonathan had left quickly and quietly had actually made her finally relax. Or maybe it was all the wonderful wine and delicious food. Or maybe all the compliments were just plain going to her fuzzy head. Or probably, she was just plain, completely exhausted.

By the time dessert was served, *everyone* was yawning. For the dessert, Terri had found a 2001 Argiolas, Isola dei Nuraghi. Being a *rare* sweet dessert wine, Terri had asked Aunt Susie's permission to use it. Getting the affirmative from her surprised aunt, Terri had prepared a vanilla gelato and instructed the servers to pour the wine over it right before serving. Over the top, they had placed gorgeous red raspberries. The result was a decadent, fabulous, dessert treat. Terri wished she wasn't so tired. Everyone enjoyed it immensely and it finished off the dinner and the evening perfectly.

Terri was also relieved to see the dinner come in at exactly three and a half hours. It was 8:30 on the nose as they all got up from the table, yawning and stretching.

"How about an after dinner drink in the basement, guys?" Uncle Bill needed to unwind and the rest of the male contingent followed him to the bottom floor. Susie, Debra, and Terri's tired cousins made their way to their rooms to prepare for an early night. Even Courtney could hardly wait to say good night, giving Jared a quick hug and kiss. The rehearsal dinner had been a complete success and tomorrow was another busy day.

Terri found herself heading to the kitchen and was stopped at the door by Angie. "Terri," she said, putting up a hand to stop her, "don't even *think* about it. Emily, Brianna, Zach, and I are going to clean everything up. Go upstairs and take a nice hot bath. You have done enough for one day." Angie didn't need to say another word.

Terri gratefully climbed the stairs to their room, more than happy to take her concerned friend's advice. A scant half an hour later, after a warm bubble bath in the luxurious bathroom, she crawled into bed and was quickly fast asleep.

Chapter 22

"**O**h, come on, Terri, wake-up!" Rico said. "You know I'll never love anyone but Sandra. How could you ever have thought we would get married?" He was laughing at her. She couldn't believe he was laughing at her!

"But Rico," Terri was begging him, "I really do love you. Can't we at least try?" He was shaking her arm now. Why was he shaking her arm?

"Terri, wake-up! Wake-up, Terri," Brianna was whispering and trying to nudge her out of a dead sleep. "Terri…….it's important, wake-up! We gotta get going."

"Uh, huh? What the hell…..?" Terri came out of her nightmare and finally saw Brianna above her with, of all things, a flashlight. Was the electricity out? "Wha……what is it, Bri? What's wrong?" Terri focused enough to see Angie getting out of bed and Angelica, also with a flashlight, helping her find shoes and a jacket. Terri reached up to attempt to turn on her bedside table lamp and Brianna stopped her.

"Don't turn on the light!" Brianna, even with a whisper, made Terri stop what she was doing.

"O.K., you two," Terri was completely awake now, "what in the hell is going on?"

"Jonathan is here and he's in the garage shuffling around for stuff, or something," Angelica said cautiously. "I was *finally* locking all the doors and setting the alarm when I saw him drive up."

"*You* were locking the doors?" Terri still was a little disoriented. "I thought that was Danielle's job."

"Yeah, well, she's asleep. So is everyone else. So let's get going," Angelica said, "before Jonathan leaves and we lose him."

"Yeah, we figure he must be heading to Cana Island," Brianna informed her confused boss. "So we decided to follow him. C'mon. Let's get moving!" She handed Terri her tennis shoes.

"Angie," Terri was astounded, "do you really think this is a good idea? What time is it anyway?" Angie just shrugged and yawned. The bedside clock said 11:25.

"We figured out that they must be meeting on Cana Island at midnight," said Brianna.

"Oh, that's original," Terri said with a laugh, as she pulled on jeans and a sweat shirt and finished tying her shoes. Angelica handed her a flashlight. "Well, you guys certainly are prepared," Terri commented, as she tried the flashlight.

"Hey, keep that light down," Angelica hissed. "We don't want Jonathan to know that we're up and, you know, on to him."

"On to him what?" Terri was still shocked that they were awake and doing anything at all. Especially since Angie had been so determined to stay out of this whole mess to start with. Obviously, her friend was *up,* for an adventure, literally, it would seem, when they should have still been peacefully slumbering. They had just barely slept enough to settle the huge meal they had just eaten *and* drank. And apparently, Brianna and Angelica hadn't slept at all!

"Just c'mon," Brianna said. "If he's *not* going to Cana Island, then we'll just turn around and come back. We'll explain on the way." She leaned out the window and looked down towards the garage. "The light just went out. I think he's leaving."

Feeling like she was in the middle of a Pink Panther movie, Terri followed Angie, Brianna, and Angelica quickly but quietly, down the stairs. The house was dead silent as they tiptoed through the living room and watched Jonathan back out of the driveway. Going out the patio doors, they waited as Angelica set the alarm. They piled into the red Chevy Blazer with Brianna at the wheel and headed toward downtown Sister Bay. It was a Friday night so there were plenty of people around. It wasn't as if they were the only ones on the road, so Jonathan probably wouldn't think it was weird that there was a vehicle behind him. Brianna left plenty of room between them, nevertheless.

"What were you guys still doing up, anyway?" Terri asked with a yawn. "I can't believe I'm even awake, much less running around in the middle of the night."

"Yeah, well I didn't have anything to drink, which, of course, is why I'm driving," Brianna said.

"Of course," Terri said, yawning again.

"Angelica couldn't sleep so we played a couple of games of pool while the guys were having after dinner drinks," Brianna continued to explain. "Then we decided to watch a movie, which just got over, like 15 minutes ago. We saw someone driving in and Angelica knew it was Jonathan's car. So we figured that as long as we were up anyway......"

"Well, *I* wasn't up, anyway," said Terri, "and neither was Angie. Which makes me wonder what you are up to, oh best friend of mine." Terri finally addressed Angie once again. "All of a sudden, out of the blue, you're all gung-ho about following Jonathan to who in the hell knows where and...."

"Cana Island, from what I gathered," Angie finally piped up, after which she just shrugged and grinned.

"Oh, that's funny," Terri said, still mystified.

"Look, he's turning on to Q," Angelica said excitedly. "He's heading to Cana Island alright. We might as well stick with him."

"I'll stay far enough back so he won't be able to see our lights," Brianna said. "We know where we're going now so I won't follow too close."

Brianna held back as Jonathan made the corner and then waited until he was out of sight to turn on to the road toward the island.

Over-Easy

She waited at the next turn until Jonathan was, once again, out of sight. By the time they made it to the pathway that led over to Cana Island, it was about 11:45. It was a bright enough night to turn off the vehicle lights before they came out of the woods. They saw Jonathan's car parked near the path and Brianna pulled in next to it. There was no sign of Jonathan, however, much to the relief of the girls.

Terri got out of the Blazer and looked toward the lighthouse. "Oh my, God," she exclaimed, "the lighthouse is lit! I can't believe it! That is so awesome!" She felt like a kid looking at a beautiful shiny toy.

"Uh, yeah. The Cana Island Lighthouse, is a working lighthouse," Angelica informed them. "Pretty cool, huh?"

"I'd say," said Brianna. "But how are we going to sneak around if the whole place is lit up?"

"We'll just stick close to the edge of the wooded area when we get to the lighthouse," said Angelica. "O.K., we can see the path without our flashlights to cross over to the island, so we'd better keep them off. At least until we get into the woods."

"You're certainly enjoying this," Terri said to Brianna. "You like a little sleuthing do you?" She suddenly tripped on a rock and Brianna grabbed her arm, keeping her on her feet.

"Are you kidding? I'm having a blast. Uh, watch your step there, Boss." Brianna firmly helped Terri right herself.

"Shhh......." said Angelica, "look you guys. I can see a small light in the woods. It must be Jonathan. We better not talk or he'll hear us for sure. Proceed quietly. Straight ahead girls."

Angelica was enjoying this, too and even though Terri thought they were all nuts she had no choice but to follow, carefully, *very carefully*, and see what would happen. She looked out to the horizon and didn't see any lights indicating a boat or any activity on the water. If someone was meeting Jonathan at midnight, how were they getting here? Running a boat with no lights, *at night?* Very dangerous and more than likely, illegal, Terri assumed. However, none of this appeared to be anything *but* illegal, so that would be the least of their concerns. Whoever *they* were, Jonathan was obviously meeting someone. From the information the girls had collected so far, it would seem that Franklin Stone and Regan, for sure, were both involved.

Finally getting across the path and to the island, the girls started to make their way through the woods. Angelica turned on her flashlight but kept it down on the ground. The path was clear but it was very dark in the wooded area. Terri couldn't help but wonder if they were trespassing in some way, shape, or form but there was no one around to stop them.

"Everyone stay close together," Angelica said low, "and just follow my light."

Finally coming out of the woods, they saw the buildings, and the lighthouse looming up out of the dark with the light shinning out into Lake Michigan. Terri couldn't believe they were doing this crazy thing but she was awestruck by the lighthouse. It was like every Nancy Drew story she had ever read, all rolled into one. And she had read a lot of them. She shook her head and tried to focus in the darkness ahead.

"Terri," Angelica was at her ear, "where was it you saw Franklin and Jonathan that first day? If someone is meeting my dopey brother here, it's probably at the same spot."

Terri looked up at the lighthouse again and tried to remember which way she had walked. That had been only four days ago but it felt like a month, so much had happened. "This way," she said moving to the right of the lighthouse but sticking close to the trees for cover. "There is a path here, between these pillars. Be careful, it's pretty rocky." They carefully followed the path, keeping their flashlights off. The light from the lighthouse was bright but barely showed the way on the path down to the water. And as if that weren't enough, the sky suddenly lit up with a sudden brilliant flash.

Terri almost screamed. "What the hell was that?"

"Shit," said Angelica, "look to the South. There's a storm coming."

"Oh, that's just perfect. You guys brought flashlights. Did you also grab some umbrellas?" Terri clung to her cousin as they heard the rumble of thunder and immediately forgot that she had been looking forward to a good thunderstorm. Suddenly the idea of being *out in it,* was not so much fun.

"Here," said Angie behind her, "put your hood up." Terri shivered as she pulled her hood up over her head. The rest of the girls followed suit. She tried to see something, *anything,* out on the water. Any kind of a vessel to show that Jonathan was here to meet someone. Where was Jonathan, anyway? She suddenly heard a thud and a grunt behind her but didn't have time to find out what it was. Another bright flash of lightening lit up the sky. Terri finally made out the shape of a craft of some sort on the horizon. Was it perhaps, **The Eclipse**, the boat she had seen that first day out on Lake Michigan? She only had time to gasp however, as a hand was clamped tightly on to her mouth and a voice behind her whispered ominously in her ear. "Who the hell are you and what are you doing here?"

Chapter 23

The rumble of thunder assaulted Terri's ears and her senses. How close was the storm? Wait for the lightening and then count the seconds, they always say. Did that mean miles or minutes? She tried to stay calm and use what she had been taught in her defense classes. Instead of fighting her attacker, she relaxed to give him a false sense of security. Balling her hands into tight fists, she pulled her arms forward for leverage. Then she quickly pushed her elbows back with a fierce jab to his ribcage and bit down hard on his hand.

"Ow, damn it!" Jonathan yelled as he released Terri and backed away from her, howling and complaining and shaking his hand. "You bit me!"

"Oh, shut up, you big stupid baby," Terri said, disgusted with him. "I told you not to mess with me, Jonathan. Serves you right!"

"I didn't know it was you," Jonathan made the excuse. Terri shrugged, so what?, and searched the darkness for the rest of the girls.

They came running up to see what had happened and now Terri looked at *them* with disgust. "And where have *you* all been? I had to rescue myself here. Thanks for nothing! All though, it was just

Jonathan, so no big thing, as it turned out." This whole business was getting ridiculous and Terri was running out of patience, *fast*. Especially with the storm coming.

"Yeah, well, thanks a lot," Jonathan said, still making a big fuss over his sore hand. "What the hell is going on here, anyway?"

"Angie fell down," Brianna informed Terri, "and skinned her knee, I'm afraid." Angelica used her flashlight to examine Angie's injuries, as they regrouped, much to the surprise of a stunned Jonathan.

"Well, when you run around in the dark, shit happens, I guess," Terri said then. "And as you can see, I found Jonathan. Poor guy, he's injured too. Aren't you glad I didn't break your arm instead like I promised, old buddy? Now, why don't we just go home, *right now*? Jonathan, you are welcome to come with us."

"Alright, all of you," Jonathan strained to gain some sense of control of the situation, "why are you here? Angelica," he suddenly saw his sister, "what are you doing here? Did you follow me?"

"Johnny, what's going on? Yeah, we followed you 'cause we are worried about you. Are you meeting that awful Franklin Stone or Regan, or what? Let us help you before something terrible happens." Angelica was pleading with her wayward brother. They were both asking questions and getting no answers. Jonathan grabbed her arms and looked at her sternly.

"Angel, please listen to me," Jonathan used his sister's childhood nick name. "This is a *very* dangerous situation. How did you guys find out about this, anyway? You shouldn't be here in the first place."

"Long story short, neither should you," Terri said then. "Jonathan, c'mon, let's just go back to the B & B. You can talk to your dad and….."

"Now please *listen* to me, all of you," Jonathan suddenly sounded mature but scared. Also, the fact that another wild bolt of lightening made them all jump didn't help any. But Jonathan went on. "I have to try to save a man's life here. I don't have a choice. They'll be coming soon."

"*Who* will be coming soon?" Angie finally spoke, even as she rubbed her injured knee. "I'm a police officer, Jonathan. Let us help you."

"You're a cop? Oh, great. That's just fabulous. Nice, Terri. You're best friend is a cop. That figures." Jonathan turned around and looked out towards the lake.

"Well, I'm a cop in Boston. Not here," Angie confessed. "But I can tell when someone needs help and if anyone needs help, that certainly would be you."

"Hey, you guys," Brianna pointed out to the east side of the lake. They all saw a light, one flash, followed by two. "There's a signal if I ever saw one," she said.

"O.K., I don't have a choice. Do you guys understand that?" Jonathan had made up his mind. "I have to go."

"Go? Go where? Go how?" Angelica was still whispering but now she was getting hysterical besides. Another rumble of thunder filled the air around them and Terri shivered again. She thought she even felt a drop of rain.

Before they could see what he was doing, Jonathan pulled a small fishing boat out from behind some bushes and pushed it over to the edge of the lake. Lowering the motor into the water, he prepared to shove off.

"Angel," he said as he ran back to them and gave his sister a tight hug, "it'll be alright, O.K.? I have to do this. If I can get it right this time, I can make up for all the stupid things I've done. You've got to let me go and finish this."

"Johnny, how will we know you're alright? What am I going to tell Mom?" Angelica was crying now and Jonathan hugged his little sister again.

"Don't tell her anything, O.K? I'll get a hold of you. Here, look." Jonathan reached into the front of his jeans and pulled out his cell phone.

"I'll call you or text you. Just wait to hear from me. You got that?" Angelica nodded as the rest of the girls watched helplessly.

Another light flashed from the boat out on the water, this time closer, followed by two more flashes.

"You guys have *got* to get out of here," Jonathan was starting to panic now. "I don't have time to argue with you anymore. Go, go now!" He started turning them all around, pushing them away, back towards the lighthouse, back to the car. Terri turned and saw Jonathan get into the boat, heard the motor start, and watched him take off into the dark.

More lightening revealed the small craft moving quickly toward the larger one. The storm was coming, the thunder rolled, and the rain started to fall. The girls ran as fast as they could, past the lighthouse, through the woods, across the rocky path, and to the Blazer. By the time they were back in the car, soaking wet and shivering with cold and fear, it was pouring down rain.

Home safe at the B & B, the girls managed to get into the house without waking the rest of the inhabitants. They had all agreed, on the drive back to Sister Bay, that there was nothing they could do but wait to hear from Jonathan. The storm was fierce and raged outside as they worried but tried to settle down and sleep. By the next morning, however, their worst fears were realized. A body had been washed up on the shore in Northport, right at the very tip of the Door County peninsula.

Chapter 24

Obviously, much to the relief of the four girls, the body washed up on the shore at Northport *was not* Jonathan. As a matter of fact, from the description of the man, no one seemed to have any idea *who* he was. Angelica had not heard from her brother, however, so they couldn't relax just yet. The storm had been a powerful one and the waves had crashed fiercely on all sides of Door County. Many speculated that this was why the body had washed up on the shore. Otherwise, it probably would have sunk into the murky waters of 'Death's Door.' This was the old timers talking, of course. Terri would have been amused if she hadn't been so concerned for Jonathan. There was definitely nothing amusing about this situation.

"What will we do now?" asked a tearful Angelica. "Johnny said he would contact me. He told me not to tell Mom anything. How do we know that *his* body didn't sink into Death's Door? Oh God, I'm just so scared." She covered her face with her hands and started to cry again.

The four girls had taken their coffee and breakfast into the basement on the premise of making room for the other guests. That actually was the case. There were still several extra people at the B &

B who would be leaving the next day to go back to Milwaukee. In the meantime, for today and tonight, the Robertson's still had a full house. Fortunately for the girls, no one noticed that they were doing anything out of the ordinary.

Brianna put her arm around Angelica, then looked to Angie and Terri for help. But it was impossible to comfort her. Until they heard from Jonathan, there was nothing any of them could do.

"Let's just give him a little more time." Terri tried to come up with any number of reasons why Jonathan had not yet called, just holding out hope that he was still alive. "He could be in a situation where he is being watched. Or maybe they took his phone away from him, whoever *they* might be, anyway. Man, I don't know what to think!" They were all at their wits end. Even Angie was having a hard time staying calm.

"Well, I don't want to think the worst here," said Angie, "but I really can't help it. That dead guy has to have something to do with whatever Jonathan was doing out there last night. It would be too much of a coincidence for the two things *not* to be connected. If we hadn't gotten caught in the rain, we may have been able to watch and see something but……"

"Well, we couldn't and we didn't," said Angelica. " We have absolutely no idea what happened out there last night. And until I hear from my brother, I am going to be a wreck," she finished, sniffling with fresh tears.

"Then I think it's time to tell your mom and dad," Terri finally came to a sensible decision. "We are running out of options here. There is no way that we can handle this without someone noticing you're upset, Angelica."

"Terri's right, Angelica," Brianna said. "It's time to get some help, no matter what Jonathan said last night. Someone is dead now, so we are past a mystery to possibly a murder. What do you think?"

Angelica didn't need to think for long. "Yeah. O.K. Let's just tell my mom and dad and get it over with. And thanks, you guys, for all of your support. None of us could have stopped Johnny from going out there last night."

"You are absolutely right, Angelica," Angie said, relieved that Terri's young cousin had made the right choice. "We have no reason to feel guilty or responsible for any of this. If we *hadn't* followed him, there maybe wouldn't even have been a chance to help, anyway. No one would have even known where he was, possibly for days. At least we have some information, sketchy at best, but it's better than nothing."

Fortunately for the four girls, Uncle Bill felt the same way. He was also very relieved. Having had no success at getting anything out of his son for the past several months, at least now he could go to the police and tell them what they knew. A dead body also meant that the feds were involved. So the girls found themselves stuck with a pretty much wasted afternoon.

Courtney, naturally, was angry with Jonathan for all the fuss he was causing. But at the same time, she was worried about him, too. "Let us know if you hear anything, Mom," she said, before she and Zack hustled Jared and her future in-laws, out of the B & B to take them for an extended ride on the **Suzie Q**, the Robertson cruiser. They would fish and get some sun. Later, they would dock somewhere along the peninsula for dinner. Hopefully, by then, there would be some news of Jonathan's whereabouts.

In the meantime, Terri, Angie, Brianna, and Angelica, were forced to answer question after question from detectives trying to piece together what had happened. First they were all questioned separately, then together, by the locals. Then they were each questioned by the Feds. Each girl had a different experience to tell. Angelica had jumped on board late in the game with Brianna somewhere in the middle.

Terri started with what she had heard and seen on Cana Island. She did not bring the, Ed and Franklin Stone aspect, into her part of the story, however. There was no reason to. Ed Stone's murder and Terri's involvement in it, had absolutely nothing to do with the present investigation. Apparently, Ed and Franklin had not been in contact with one another for some time. Franklin, at the moment, was also still unaccounted for. Had he been pushed into Lake Michigan by Regan? And speaking of Regan, where was *she*? Terri tried to ask the federal agent who was jotting down notes on her story some questions of her own. True to form, however, the authorities never offered any answers. They only wanted them.

"Now, Ms. Springee, let's go over your story one more time." The federal agent addressed Terri once again, pronouncing the silent *e* at the end of her name, making her bristle.

"Excuse me," said Emily, who was standing by, "that's Springe, not Springee...., the e is silent. And I don't think I like your tone, Agent, whatever *your* name is." Emily had been kept out of the loop all this time and she was very testy. But *nothing*, made her more ticked off, than to hear the last name she had boasted for nearly 35 years, pronounced incorrectly. It wasn't as if the man hadn't been told. Terri grinned in spite of herself. The guy looked as if he was being scolded by his own mom. It wasn't like this was easy for him either.

"Grisham," said the detective. "Agent Bob Grisham." Uh oh, thought Terri, here we go.

"Now listen here, Grissom," said Emily, "I think we've all had just about enough of this. You have been questioning my daughter, her friends, and my niece for hours. Isn't it about time you got back out into the field, as they say, and start this investigation *away* from this house? Find out who your vic is, then you'll know who to question next." Emily had definitely been watching way too much C.S.I. Terri had to bite her lip now to keep from laughing hysterically. Where was Gil Grissom when they needed him?

"It's Grisham, ma'am," said the young detective, "like the author, not the guy on T.V."

"Fine," said Emily, and then Terri knew for sure that her mother had done it on purpose. "I don't care what your name is. You've asked enough questions. It's time to move on."

"She's right, detective," now Angie piped up putting in her two cents worth. "I'm a City of Boston police officer and I know the 'good cop, bad cop' routine pretty well. I agree with Mrs. Springe. Time to move on. You've inconvenienced this family long enough. And, by the way, also keep in mind, that you have been questioning these people without their lawyer present. I think they have been more than accommodating."

"Well, we don't care if you *are* a city of Boston cop or not," said the other agent who had introduced himself as Reynolds. Then, deliberately avoiding Angie's reference to a lawyer, he added, "This ain't no tea party, officer. This is an investigation on a federal level. Now we could have a murder on our hands here and…."

"Murder? Who said anything about murder anyway?" Angelica had definitely reached her limit too. "How do we know this idiot didn't just fall overboard and drown? There hasn't been time for an autopsy. They just found him this morning."

"Tea party?" Angie was appalled. "What is it with everyone thinking that we have one huge-assed, on-going, tea party in Boston? Now you guys are just pissing me off!"

"Mr. Robertson," Reynolds, of course, ignored Angelica and Angie to address Bill, "have you noticed any antiques, drugs, or other precious items missing from your home, as of late?"

"Now wait just a minute here," Sue jumped in, "you are *not* insinuating that our son Jonathan, would have stolen anything from his own home?"

"I wasn't insinuating anything, ma'am. Just answer the question, sir," stated Reynolds to Bill. Now *Sue* was pissed.

"He will do no such thing, pal…."she said, and then suddenly everyone started talking at once.

"Now calm down, Susie," Bill tried to contain his wife's temper.

"Try to be nice and professional and what does it get you? Insults!" Angie groused.

"I'm tired and I want to go back to bed," complained Brianna like a ten year old. "Some vacation this is!"

"My brother hasn't called me yet and until he does….," Angelica was whining and started crying again.

Terri was astonished at how out of control the situation had suddenly gotten. The detectives were being completely intimidated by the Robertson family and their guests. And why did she hear musical notes? What was that? It sounded like a show tune, or a doorbell, or a….

"Hey, everybody, stop!" Terri stood up. The room actually quieted down and the musical sound filled the air. "Angelica, it's your phone," Terri said.

"Oh, my God," Angelica grabbed her phone from a nearby end table and saw who it was. "Johnny!" Angelica was crying, this time with happiness, as she *finally* heard her brother's voice. Then the whole room exploded again.

Chapter 25

Terri was relieved by how quiet it was now. She sat on the pier, in the dark, all by herself. Angie had practically pushed her out the door to relax alone for a bit.

"Try to just take it easy for awhile," her friend had calmly advised Terri. "This has been one helluva ride. I'll join you a little bit later. K?"

So Terri had grabbed a sweater, even though it was a beautiful evening, along with a glass of wine. Now she was sitting, listening to the calm shooshing sound of the waves lapping up on the beach. It was very weird as she remembered where she had been, just one short week ago. She and Rico had been on their wonderful date. Well, *that* certainly had ended badly. In less than one week later, she and her friends, and eventually even her mother, had gotten involved in a full-blown mystery. They still had a week left of their vacation, though. Terri was thankful for that. Maybe now they could actually relax and enjoy themselves. Door County had so much to offer and they had hardly seen any of it in the five days they had been there.

Jonathan had finally called from a Milwaukee County jail. It certainly had taken him long enough. In the confusion of a busy

Milwaukee Saturday of criminal activity, they had indeed taken his phone and other personal property. By the time it was returned to him, he knew his family would be frantic. The initial relief, however, was followed by dozens of questions. Yes, he was alright. No, he didn't know where Regan or Franklin was. Regan, as it turned out, was with the Feds. She had been recruited by them seven months before, to find out what was going on with Jonathan and Franklin. Franklin Stone had been stealing antiques and prescription drugs from customers, especially old, wealthy customers he and Jonathan had been doing odd jobs for, over the past year. Regan was an old friend and Jonathan had trusted her. Courtney was, of course, overjoyed that *her* friend Regan was not a criminal after all.

Jonathan, on the other hand, had gotten involved with moving the stolen items out of The Door, with Franklin Stone running the show. When he had reached **The Eclipse** the night before, Regan and Franklin were on board, along with a criminal hook-up from Canada named Gerard Simmons. The authorities had been trying to get their hands on Simmons for quite some time. That had been the actual plan. Unfortunately, at least for the authorities, it was *his* body that had washed up on the beach at Northport, at the tip of Door County. He and Franklin had gotten into an argument. The ship had been tossed about in the waves during the storm. A fight had ensued and they had *both* fallen off of **The Eclipse.** Regan was left with no choice but to tell Jonathan what was going on and call the Coast Guard to rescue them. Rescue for Jonathan had meant immediate arrest, but at the time, it was preferable to death. Franklin had been nowhere to be found and it was impossible to search for him during the storm. Old as he was, it was doubtful that he would have survived. It would have been nearly impossible for *anyone* to survive in the water, under the circumstances.

Terri found the whole incident to be bizarre and filled with irony. What a terrible end to the life of Franklin Stone, much like his brother Ed. They could have had a relationship as brothers and led fairly normal lives. But they had both made the wrong choices and met with tragic deaths. No one was using the word murder anymore. Both Regan and Jonathan had told the same story. Along with the storm and their greed, Gerard Simmons and Franklin Stone had controlled their own destinies, in the end. Unfortunately, the authorities had wanted to capture Simmons alive, as he would have possibly led them to a larger circle of thieves. But Simmons was dead and Franklin was assumed dead.

Jonathan's fate was left in the hands of a good lawyer and eventually, a judge. Terri assumed some jail time would be involved. Perhaps after serving his time, he could pick up the pieces and go on to make wiser decisions. She certainly hoped so. Terri had seen good in Jonathan and believed that he had really wanted to try to save Franklin Stone's life.

Regan had done what she could, to fulfill her assignment but resolved to stay out of the under cover world in the future. Case closed. At least here in Door County, Wisconsin.

Terri took a sip of her wine and sighed, finally feeling the frustration of the last few days fall off of her shoulders. Hearing footsteps behind her, she put her wine down. "Hey, Angie," she said without turning around, "I was starting to get lonely out here.

"It's not Angie," Rico said simply, making Terri jump up and turn around to see him walking towards her. She shook her head as if to clear her brain.

"Am I dreaming again?" Terri asked. Rico reached down and picked up her hand. He took it in both of his and tenderly kissed her shaking fingers. Terri closed her eyes and felt the warmth of his breath, and took in the wonderful scent of his skin, his hair.

"I'm here, finally," he said with a catch in his throat, "and I am so very sorry, sorry, sorry, for any pain I may have caused you. I have been an idiot and it's time to tell you why."

"I wish you would," Terri felt like crying but she didn't want to. She wanted to keep her senses and understand. And she wanted to save her strength. "I really need to know what has been happening to you. Do you want to tell me now?"

"Yes, but let's sit down." Still holding her hand, Rico moved them both over to the bench on the pier and they sat close together. He put his other arm around her but still didn't let go of her hand. Terri laughed a little.

"You can let go of my hand," she said, with a shaky laugh, "I'm not going anywhere."

"We'll talk about that in a little while. First I'll tell you my story. O.K?"

Terri nodded and Rico started to talk.

When Rico and Sandra had met, obviously it was under very emotional circumstances. The one thing everyone had in common back then was the terrorist attacks. But they had fallen in love. Rico had felt it was right and was as sure as he could be that Sandra was the woman he wanted to spend the rest of his life with. They quickly became engaged and, like any other normal couple, began to make their wedding plans. Rico had also loved Sandra's family very much. He had become extremely close to her parents, Sylvia and Albert. Sandra and Cheryl were their only children and he was, typically, the son they had always wanted.

"Two weeks before the wedding, Sandra and Cheryl came to my office." Rico was stumbling over the words now and Terri could tell it was more painful than she could have ever imagined.

"Put simply, Sandra had changed her mind," he choked on the words. "She wanted to cancel our wedding. She took off her engagement ring and placed it on my desk. Considerate of her at the time, I guess." Terri gasped but didn't comment.

"She had found someone else. A doctor, of course. She was a nurse, after all. They're surrounded by good-looking doctors. She had fallen for one of them and they were having an affair." Rico finally let go of Terri's hand at this point and brought his hands together at his knees.

"You don't have to go on with this," Terri said then, touching his shoulder. "I know how it ends."

"No, no you don't," Rico was anxious to go on, "there is so much more."

"O.K." Terri said and waited.

"Sandra had brought Cheryl with her, to keep me from blowing my top at her. That was obvious. So when they left my office together, I could never have imagined what would happen after that." Rico looked down at his hands and kept talking. "Yes, as you may have already figured out, they were killed in a car wreck that very afternoon, after they left me."

Terri wasn't sure she could handle this much suffering from Rico. This was so much worse than she had ever imagined. And she had said all of those awful things to him the night before she left for Door County. Oh, no. Now she felt like the jerk in this story. But Rico wasn't done.

"Sandra and Cheryl's parents were devastated beyond belief," he went on, his voice breaking. "Sylvia had a stroke shortly after hearing of the accident. It was as if they had lost everything. Their daughters were dead and now they would lose me, too."

Terri nodded. She could come up with no words of comfort.

"All of those times when I just up and left, without explanation? It was because of Sylvia. I was all she had. She was suffering terribly. The hospital and eventually a nursing facility Albert had moved her to in Boston, would call me when she was at her worst. All I could do was try to calm her. I was the only one she wanted to see. " He drew one last breath. "She finally died a couple of months ago. What a blessing that has been!"

"Um, ah, what happened to Sandra's father, Albert?" Terri couldn't help but ask the question. Might as well fill in all the gaps.

"You wouldn't believe it. Tough bastard," Rico laughed a little. "Found himself another lady, almost right away. I guess it was his way of coping. Kind of left me in the lurch though. What could I do? Sylvia was never going to recover. Albert went to visit her often, too, but she seemed to feel that I was suffering as much as she was. Seeing me made her feel closer to her daughter, I guess." Rico brought his hands together up by his mouth and looked out at the bay. "It really is nice here," he finally commented.

"Yeah, it is, isn't it?" Terri welcomed the break in Rico's terrible story. "In the last week or so, since we got here, I thought about you so much, Rico. I thought about how much you would enjoy it here." She sucked in her breath and made an attempt at her own apology. "I'm sorry, too. I shouldn't have lost my temper that last night, before I left. I just was so confused."

"No, it's O.K.," Rico looked at her now and gently touched her cheek. "I just couldn't bring myself to tell you, or anyone else for that matter. It was just such a humiliating and bizarre story. You can't believe how many times I blamed myself. Why did Sandra find someone else? What did I do wrong or *not* do right? So, then, here I was, pushing you away. What an idiot I've been."

Terri sat for a few minutes, trying to come up with the right words. This was a tough one. What now? She had to ask one more thing, and hopefully, they could move on from there. "Um, Rico," she was unsure how to word it, "are you like, um, you know, over her? Can you and I move ahead without her or what happened, *ever* being an issue? Is that going to be a lot to ask?"

"No, as a matter of fact," Rico said, and Terri breathed a sigh of relief. "As hurt as I was when Sandra and Cheryl walked out the door of my office, I was more angry with her for not, at least being honest with me and just moving on sooner. She had been involved with this guy for months and kept making our wedding plans. What was she going to do? Marry me and keep him on the side?" Terri had no comment for such a weird scenario. Rico went on. "You can't believe, though, how weird it was to be at that funeral. There were hundreds of people and they all thought that I was the one who needed to be comforted the most. It really sucked! All I could do was make my way through it and then try to get the hell on with my life somehow. But then there was Sylvia to deal with."

"Yeah, I think I know what you mean." Terri thought for a second. "That would be one of those surreal situations, where you're there but not really there-there. Like an 'out of body experience,' that kind of thing." Terri couldn't help but come up with something her sisters might say. Rico actually laughed at that and it seemed to help clear the air.

"Yeah, something like that," Rico said, "but I want to forget about all of that now. Oh, and by the way, there's just one more thing." Rico wanted to make sure he left nothing out. "After we got engaged, Sandra and I both took out life insurance policies for $1 million each, you know, because of 9/11." Now, Terri gasped again.

"She actually *forgot* to take my name off of the policy or I would assume she was going to take care of it eventually."

" Holy shit!" Terri couldn't help herself. "You got that money?"

"I sure did," Rico now seemed pleased with himself. "Part of it was used to take care of the funerals and some of Sylvia's medical bills. But a lot of it was invested and I think I've actually done pretty well."

"Do not tell me you are rich!" Terri said. "I can not stand it!"

"Fine," said Rico, now with a big grin, "I won't tell you then. I mean, I'm no Donald Trump but….."

"Thank God for that," Terri said, smiling and touching his beautiful, soft dark hair. And oh, it smelled so good!

"So, anyway," Rico went on, wasting no more time with the past, "I have a question that I need to ask you right now. Are you ready?"

Could it be? Was this for real? Terri held her breath and waited. Rico didn't move, he just took her hand again and pulled her close.

"Terri Lyn Springe," he said, very formally but very quietly, "I love you, very, very much. I can say that with complete confidence." At this, Terri sighed with relief again as Rico went on. "So, would you please, *please*, consent to be my wife?"

"Rico David Mathews, I love you, too, very much." Rico smiled then, as Terri answered him, her voice shaking, "I would love to be your wife. And I promise you now, that I will *not* change my mind. Not ever!"

Chapter 26

Terri sat in the bay window back in her little apartment in Boston. Louie was on one side of her and Maria was on the other. The two fluffy kitties had definitely missed her. They had refused to leave her side for days. The window was open and they were enjoying what would probably be the last of the really nice fall weather. Winter was coming, making the air smell sharp and the days get shorter. In a few days the girls would be moving into their new apartment above 'Terri's Table.' Of course, Terri would be making her home with Rico Mathews next summer, *after* they were married.

For about the millionth time, Terri Springe looked at her beautiful engagement ring. As soon as they had gotten back to Boston, Terri and Rico had picked the ring out. Rico knew Terri would want to do this important thing together. But he also insisted that she not even think about the price, so she didn't. After a minimal amount of deliberation, she chose a perfect one caret diamond surrounded by small sapphires. The wedding band slipped underneath the setting of the diamond and sapphires, blending into a gorgeous set of rings of gold with the sparkling stones over the top. Rico's matching wedding band, also contained diamonds and sapphires. Then, that

Then finally, there was the wedding! It had rained in the morning, making them all anxious about the arrangements to have the wedding outside. But like so often happens on days like this one, it had cleared up, the sun came out, and the rain left everything fresh and sparkly clean. Courtney, looking radiant and happy, walked down the stairs and out the French doors, down the steps, and up into the gazebo to Jared's side, just as Terri had imagined it. The girls followed in their beautiful dresses, with matching jewelry, shoes, and clutch purses.

Many other relatives turned up for the wedding and they all enjoyed getting reacquainted. Terri's sisters, Rachel and Becca arrived on the Thursday before the wedding and were relieved that Rico was there and thrilled about the engagement. Terri had called her father, who had relayed his congratulations by phone. She had also e-mailed her brother Rob, informing him that Terri and Rico's, was one wedding he would not be able to get out of!

The one hundred guests or so, milled around and enjoyed the view, as the wedding party mingled, with drinks in hand, laughing and talking. The rest of the wonderful champagne, sent by David Severson, was served, as well as soda, beer, and in true Wisconsin tradition, wine coolers.

A buffet of appetizers was arranged and was more than substantial to be an early afternoon meal. The caterer kept the buffet supplied through out the party after the short ceremony. They served a full crisp and colorful salad bar, fresh fruits and veggies, with dips, more cheeses, and assorted crackers, meatballs, in a savory gravy, chicken wings and drummies, with assorted sauces, cocktail wieners, bacon wrapped chestnuts, and baked beans, another Wisconsin tradition. There was also a beautiful cake! A fabulous, creamy, raspberry swirl in white cake, with a whipped cream frosting concoction that melted in their mouths.

"Oh, yum," said Angie, after her third piece. "Now I can die happy."

"Just wait until mine and Terri's wedding, Angie," said Rico, as he squeezed his fiance's hand. "When we get back to Boston, we're *both* going on diets."

Terri never would have imagined that she could be so happy.

Over-Easy

The door opening and closing got Terri's attention. She turned and smiled at Brianna. Maria and Louie jumped down to greet her. Absentmindedly scooping up Maria, Brianna plopped down on the sofa next to the window and took Terri's hand, thoughtfully running her fingers over the beautiful engagement ring.

"I can only hope, that someday, I will be as happy as you are at this very moment, Terri. You'll miss us though, right? What will I do without you?" Terri squeezed Brianna's hand and felt herself tearing up.

"Aw c'mon, we'll see each other at the shop everyday, Sweetie," Terri tried to sooth her young friend. "I'm getting old. I can't wait too much longer, if I'm going to give Emily that grandchild she wants so much." She laughed a little but she felt as sentimental as Brianna right now. Why did it seem like they had known each forever? Sometimes, chance friendships were like that. This one certainly was.

"Yeah, you're right," Brianna said, "I suppose I should start thinking about making some plans for my own future. Now that my mother and father are getting divorced, I need to get my head on straight. I'm really glad for my dad, though. He deserves some happiness and he can not have a happy life with my mother. She will never get well, plain and simple."

Terri didn't comment on this statement or try to convince Brianna that it would change. She was right. Elizabeth would not get well, which had finally led David Severson to make the choice he had. He needed to be free of Elizabeth and go on with his own life.

"Want some tea? It's getting chilly." Terri nodded and Brianna went to the kitchen and started getting out tea things. She would serve the tea with buttery tea biscuits, cream, sugar, and lemon, using pretty, delicate cups and saucers.

Yes, I will miss this, Terri thought. But I have to move on. On to a new life as Mrs. Rico Mathews. Next summer, I will become Mrs. Rico Mathews and then everything will be perfect.

To be continued……………..

Recipes For Over-Easy

Stuffed Mushrooms

1 12-oz package of fresh mushrooms (see note)
1 cup of soft bread crumbs (plain or Italian)
½ stick of butter (more if needed for sautéing)
3-4 green onions (or dried chives)
6 cooked medium shrimp (thaw, if frozen)
1 tsp. of cumin or curry (or ½ tsp. of ea.)
1 tsp. salt
½ tsp. pepper
Dried parsley and paprika for garnish (over cooked mushrooms)
Olive oil cooking spray

    In a medium bowl, mix together breadcrumbs and spices.
    Very lightly rinse mushrooms or wipe off any residue, with a soft damp cloth. **Do not** soak mushrooms in water, they are like sponges. Trim any dried or dirty ends off of stems. Remove stems from caps, keeping caps in intact. Chop stems into small pieces. Thinly slice green onions, using all of white part and about a half inch of green part. Chop thawed shrimp into small pieces. Melt butter in medium sauce pan and sauté chopped mushroom stems, onions, and shrimp, on medium heat for about 5 minutes. **Do not burn!** Add more butter if necessary. You want enough of the hot mixture to add to breadcrumbs, so it will be moist enough, like any kind of stuffing. Mix breadcrumbs and spices together with butter mixture. Spray

cookie sheet with olive oil. Place empty mushrooms caps on tray and fill each cap with stuffing mixture.

Bake in 350 degree oven, until the mushrooms begin to brown and sizzle, about 20 minutes. Sprinkle with paprika and parsley. Serve immediately!

Author's note: I like a variety of sizes for these delicious stuffed mushrooms to make them more of a finger food. However, you can buy the large variety especially for stuffing. For those you may need a knife and fork!

Also for a variation, you can use crab or even lobster meat, instead of shrimp. And if you use dried chives, instead of green onions, they will not need to be sautéed. Just add to the dry ingredients. Also, **do not** use margarine instead of butter!

Twice-Baked Potatoes

6 Large Russet potatoes
1-16 carton of sour cream
1 stick of butter (again, no substitutions)
Approx. 1 T. of dried chives
2 tsp. of garlic salt
1 tsp. of pepper
Paprika and parsley for garnish

Scrub potatoes well. Poke holes in **top** of potatoes, place on oven rack in middle of oven, and bake in 350 oven, for about an hour. Check with knife before removing from oven, to make sure that potatoes are completely cooked. Remove from oven and allow to cool for about 15 minutes, just long enough to be able to handle them, without burning your fingers. Slice top off of cooked potatoes, lengthwise, about a ½ inch. Scoop cooked potato into a large bowl, leaving the bottom of shells intact. Also, scrape as much of potato off of tops as you can and dispose of skin from the tops. Using a handheld potato masher, mash cooked potato, cutting in chunks of butter. Add garlic salt and pepper. Continue to mash potatoes. Add sour cream and mash together, to get a nice consistency. The mixture will be lumpy, you want it that way. Taste and adjust seasonings. Fill potato shells with mixture. Pile mixture high in shells.(These potatoes can be prepared the day before you serve them and kept in the fridge until being baked again before the meal.)
   Bake in 350 degree oven, until tops of potatoes start to brown. Brush with melted butter and sprinkle with paprika and parsley.
   For variations, sprinkle with shredded cheese, or mix cheese in mashed potato mixture before re-cooking. You can also add bacon bits or broccoli florets or both!

Mushroom and Rice Soup

1-12 oz. package of fresh mushrooms
3-4 tablespoons of margarine
1 medium white onion
3 tablespoons of flour
5-6 cups of chicken broth
A 'handful' of baby carrots (sliced into small pieces)
½ cup of long grain rice
2 Bay leaves
Dried parsley to sprinkle on top of soup (about a tablespoon)

Lightly rinse any dirt residue off of mushrooms, or lightly clean with a damp cloth. Cut off any dried or dirty ends of mushroom stems. Remove stems from mushrooms. Chop mushroom stems, carrots, and onion and sauté in melted margarine in large pot. Sprinkle flour over sautéed vegetables and stir together. The flour, margarine, and veggies will form a thick, pasty mixture. Slice mushroom caps and add to pot, still stirring mixture. Add more margarine if desired, to sauté sliced mushroom tops. Slowly add chicken broth, continuing to stir. Add rice and bay leaves, still stirring as soup comes to a boil. Sprinkle with dried parsley. Turn down soup to medium and cover, with lid slightly off of pot, to let out steam. If desired, add diced chicken. This can be either leftover cooked chicken or a cooked, chopped chicken breast. Allow soup to boil, until veggies are cooked and rice is split and tender. The flour will thicken the soup. If more broth is desired, you can always add another cup of water, with a chicken bouillon cube, or a tsp. of chicken broth granules.

Serve with crisp saltines, sliced meats, and cheeses.

The next two recipes are contingent on a large bone-in ham, anywhere from six to seven pounds, from which you will get three meals. For your first meal, cook the ham until sizzling hot, slice, and serve with mashed potatoes, your choice of vegetables, and warm rolls, for one meal. Your next meal is:

Creamy Scalloped Potatoes and Ham

Peel and slice enough potatoes, your choice, reds or russets, to fill a large oval roaster. I have made scalloped potatoes and ham for family gatherings, in that case filling the largest blue roaster. For your family, you might wish to use a medium blue roaster.

Slice one medium onion, add to potatoes in roaster. Salt potatoes and onions, depending on your dietary needs. You can always taste, adding salt and pepper, after this dish is cooked.

Dice leftover ham, enough to cover potatoes in roaster. Dot potatoes, ham, and onions, with pats of margarine, about one stick. Pour 2% milk over ingredients, enough to almost cover, leaving about an inch from the top. You may have some spill over, as milk boils rather hard. Roaster can be placed on a large cookie sheet, to catch any boiled over milk, or you can cover the bottom of your oven, with aluminum foil for easy clean-up. You want your potatoes to be nice and tender, so this dish should be cooked about and hour and a half, at 350 degrees.

When potatoes are tender, thicken milk with a couple of tablespoons of corn starch, dissolved in warm water, if desired. This yummy meal stands alone but you may wish to add a can of any vegetables you desire, on the side, along with warm rolls. Enjoy on a chilly night!

Your next meal is:

Ham and Bean Soup

1 lb. (bag) of Navy Beans
1 ham bone, leftover of course, from your cooked ham (hopefully with some ham left on it, to add to soup)
1 4 oz. can of tomato sauce
1 medium chopped onion
1 cup or so of chopped celery
1 cup of chopped carrot
1 large can of chicken broth
2 or 3 Bay leaves
2 or 3 medium potatoes
Additional chicken broth or water

    The best part about this recipe? It all goes into your medium blue roaster, and into the oven! Yes, bean soup in the oven. No more worrying about burning your soup. You don't even have to soak the beans. Just lightly rinse beans in a strainer, dump into roaster, add ham bone, broth, onion, bay leaves, celery, tomato sauce, and carrot pieces and cover. This soup cooks all day, at 350 degrees. Check periodically and add water or more broth as beans cook and soak up liquid. About two hours before you plan to serve soup, add chopped potatoes.
    Serve with crisp saltines, meats, and cheeses.

The only way to prepare lobster tails!

Authors' note: I normally prepare 5 lobster tails for my family. I *used* to make them in boiling water. But no more! Working in a restaurant for 7 years, showed me a better way. I pretty much described it in the text, as Terri and Danielle were preparing them. But here is the step-by-step directions, anyway.

5 Frozen Lobster tails-about 10-12 oz. each
White wine
Lemon juice
Butter
Lemon slices
Paprika
Dried or fresh parsley

Your lobster tails **must** be thawed. They should be left to thaw in the fridge, for two to three days. It will be easy to tell if they are completely thawed, as you will be able to bend them and work with them. As I described in the text, taking the thawed tail in your left hand (or right, if you are left-handed), using a kitchen shears, carefully cut down the back of the shell, to the tail, as far as you can, without removing the meat from the shell. Carefully take the meat out of the shell, bring the sides of the empty shell together, fanning the meat out over the top of the shell. Place your prepared lobsters, in a 9x13 cake pan, with about an inch of water. Splash white wine and lemon juice over the raw tails. Cook lobsters in a 350 degree oven for anywhere from 20-30 minutes, depending on how big they are. When your lobster meat is nice and white and no longer translucent, they are done. Brush with hot melted butter, sprinkle with paprika and dried (or fresh parsley) if desired. Serve with extra melted butter on the side.

Having mentioned in my first book, 'Spaghetti W/Murder,' the chef who gave me the simple recipe for making a delicious pork loin, I learned this way of cooking lobsters, from my friend and the a really great chef, that I worked with, Edward (Ned) Hagen. I still miss you Ned and hope you are doing O.K.

Bonus Recipe from Bev Grenawalt (my editor and friend)

Fabulously Moist Rhubarb Cake

1 Yellow Cake mix
3 cups of chopped rhubarb (peeled, if desired)
1 ½ cups of sugar
½ pint of whipping cream

    Following the instructions on cake mix box, pour cake batter into 9x13 cake pan. Mix cut-up rhubarb with sugar. Pour over unbaked cake mix in the pan. Pour whipping cream (in liquid form, do not whip the cream) over all.
    Bake according to instructions on cake mix box. The rhubarb sinks to the bottom of the cake mix and the whipping cream makes it 'fabulously moist.'
    This cake is so awesome, you can serve and enjoy it all by itself. Or you could add a scoop of ice cream, or top it with whipped cream, or another cut up fruit, like strawberries, or blueberries, or add chopped nuts. It is so delicious and simple to make and you won't be able to resist it! Enjoy!

<u>Teaser</u> (from the author)

In my last book DOUBLE TRUFFLE,
I promised the following recipes:

The Perfect Prime Rib
Meat Balls in Beef Gravy
Grandma's Hot Turkey Sandwiches
Rocky River Bottom (cream cheese-pudding torte)
………..many more!

Different circumstances made me use different recipes,
so I will save the above ones for my next book,
Kill Dill (Vol. 1), and yes, there will be a
Kill Dill (Vol. 2).

Thanx for reading OVER-EASY!